Books by Natalie Kleinman
in the Linford Romance Library:

AFTER ALL THESE YEARS
SAFE HARBOUR

THE GHOST OF GLENDALE

Phoebe Marcham is resigned to spinsterhood, unwilling to settle for less than the deep love her parents shared. Then adventurer Duncan Armstrong rides into her home wood, with laughter in his eyes and more charm in his little finger than anyone she has ever met before. Far from ridiculing her family ghost, Duncan resolves to help solve the mystery that has left Simon Marcham soul in torment for two hundred years. Will they be able to put the ghost to rest — and find love together?

NATALIE KLEINMAN

THE GHOST
OF GLENDALE

Complete and Unabridged

LINFORD
Leicester

First published in Great Britain in 2018

First Linford Edition
published 2018

A catalogue record for this book is available
from the British Library.

ISBN 978–1–4448–3749–0

Published by
F. A. Thorpe (Publishing)
Anstey, Leicestershire

Set by Words & Graphics Ltd.
Anstey, Leicestershire
Printed and bound in Great Britain by
T. J. International Ltd., Padstow, Cornwall

This book is printed on acid-free paper

1

'Ah, you are home at last. And how did you find your mother's relations?'

'All are well, Papa, and send their respects. Clarissa looked as happy as any bride should and my aunt was in the best of spirits, particularly as the Prince Regent chose to put in an appearance at the wedding breakfast. A feather in her cap, even though his popularity has waned of late.'

'Well I have no time for such pretensions and I'm glad to have you back. Mrs Wiggins drives me to distraction with her fussing. Yes, come in, woman,' he said as the object of his rant entered with a tray. The two were not as at odds as they appeared, there being a fondness on both sides after so many years' association. Each turned to protest as Phoebe folded back the blinds to open a window.

'The heat is far too intense outside,' Edward complained. 'Would you have me faint from suffocation?'

'Nonsense, Papa. It is much cooler this late in the day, and you have never fainted in your life. A little fresh air will do you good,' she remarked as a gentle breeze relieved the oppression. 'I've only been away for two weeks and already the place feels stuffy and unlived in,' she added, though her smile took the edge from her words.

'Now don't you go fussing, miss. Your father can't abide the heat, as well you know.' The old retainer had come into Somerset from the capital upon the marriage of her late mistress and did not live by the maxim that country air was good for one. 'And the shutters have been pulled to keep out the sun, so what would be the point?'

'The point would be to bring some light into these old rooms. I swear this dark panelling makes me feel as if I had come not from a wedding but a funeral.'

'Don't say so, Miss Phoebe. 'Tis unlucky,' the old woman said, glancing nervously over her shoulder.

'Be done with your superstitions. Come, let us leave Papa in peace.'

They closed the door behind them and Mrs Wiggins turned to Phoebe, all concern. 'What do you think, miss? He does fret so when you're away.'

Phoebe looked down fondly at Mrs Wiggins, remembering the times when she'd craned her neck to look up to her mother's old nurse; measuring back to back with her as the years went by; shrieking with joy when she became taller and then wondering if she would ever stop growing. By the time she did, she stood a willowy five feet seven inches in her stockinged feet.

'There's plenty of fight in him yet, Mrs Wiggins. Faint from suffocation indeed,' she said with a laugh, and went to put off her travelling clothes. 'I shall not keep you long tonight, for I mean to be up early in the morning to ride,' she told her abigail. 'Nothing will rid me of these fidgets quicker than a good canter, and I aim to be out before breakfast while it will still be pleasantly cool.'

'Yes, ma'am,' the young girl said, adjusting Phoebe's dress before she went to join her father.

Phoebe was the child of Edward Marcham's old age. At twenty-four years old, she was his delight and his reason for living after the untimely demise of his wife some twelve years earlier. That delight showed on his wrinkled face as she entered the dining room and bestowed an affectionate salute upon his forehead before seating herself at the table.

'Tell me then about all your jaunting around in London.'

Phoebe laughed. 'You well know that while I enjoy an occasional trip to the capital, my heart is here at Glendale. I spent far more on frills and furbelows than was wise, but my one real extravagance was that I have ordered a new riding habit, for mine is looking quite shabby.'

'Well that comes as no surprise, for you are often seen to be in the saddle.' But he was pleased she felt as he did about the old house. 'Young Brendon visited while you were away,' he added casually, for he had long hoped for an alliance between his daughter and the son of his closest friend and neighbour.

'Well I am glad you had some company. No, don't look at me like that. You should know that Rupert and I, while remaining the best of friends, have no desire to form an alliance just to satisfy the whim of yourself and his father. I wish you will not keep bringing this matter up,' Phoebe said, a touch of steel in her voice.

'I merely commented that he had visited. You are too quick to make assumptions,' he said, the timbre of his voice matching her own.

She apologised immediately. 'You are right, and I beg pardon. I am weary after my journey and should not have spoken so.'

Edward sighed inwardly. Though his dearest wish was to keep his daughter close, he longed to see her established. At her age, the prospect of her achieving a happy marriage seemed more remote than ever.

'Perhaps it would be well for you to retire then,' he said gently. 'I am tired myself. Will I see you at breakfast?'

Phoebe smiled, for she hated to be at odds with her father. 'You shall, Papa, but not before I have had a good gallop. Then I shall truly know I am home.'

* * *

A good night's sleep did much to restore Phoebe's good humour. She was not unmindful of her situation, but she remembered the affection in which her parents had held each other. Nothing would induce her to settle for less, and she had long ago concluded she was destined to remain a spinster. She could see no clear way forward and did not allow herself to dwell on the problem.

Marriage with Rupert, even had he been willing, would secure her future, but she would not be untrue to herself, nor indeed to him.

'Good morning, Will,' Phoebe said as she entered the stable yard which lay to the back of the main house. 'How have the horses been coping in this fierce heat?'

'Better'n me, miss, for sure. Me and the boys, we've been exercising them early, or later in the evening when it's cooled down a bit. Some of 'em are out even now, you'll see.'

'Not with Jester, I hope.'

'No, we'd heard you were home and made certain we'd see you here first thing this morning. Jester is saddled up and ready for you.'

'I'll be off then before the sun rises any higher, and let him have a run under cover of the trees. Ah, good day, young man,' she said fondly as Jester appeared, then laughed as he nudged her gently with his muzzle. Phoebe jumped into the saddle and they headed for the relative cool of the home wood.

'I think that's enough for the time being,' Phoebe murmured some time later, dismounting and loosening the girth. 'We shall both walk from here. Yes, I know my pace is slow for you,' she remarked as the gelding pulled forward, 'but you must for once match your steps to mine.'

Reaching a small clearing, she drew the rein over Jester's head and sat on a fallen tree to enjoy her surroundings. The horse waited patiently, nosing the ground with interest and sending the dust flying with the air from his nostrils, causing Phoebe to laugh aloud.

'Ah, another human being,' said a disembodied voice, startling her into silence as she jumped to her feet to identify the intruder. 'Had you not laughed, I might have turned in another direction and missed you completely. I am entirely lost and throw myself upon your mercy.'

The voice, unmistakably Scottish,

belonged to a man who appeared through the trees mounted on a very large chestnut. She watched him with open curiosity as he too dismounted and drew nearer, hair darker than her own and with hazel eyes that were flecked with green. 'Duncan Armstrong at your service,' he said with a deep bow and, upon straightening up and with a gleam in his eye, 'though I am hoping it will be the other way around.'

'Phoebe Marcham, sir, and I should like you to know that you are trespassing.'

'I feared as much,' he said ruefully, fingering his chin and failing completely to look contrite. 'Beau and I have been out now for two hours, and I am becoming concerned for him. I came out early in the hope of missing the worst of the heat.'

This was something Phoebe was well able to appreciate. Had she not done the same? 'How came you to be so far off track? You are not local. I would know you if you were.'

'Far from local. My land lies north of the border, though it is some time since I have been home. My brother runs things there. Shall we sit?' he asked, gesturing to the place she had vacated.

'I thought you were anxious for your horse?'

'So I am,' he said, 'but it is cool enough here and easier to talk than when walking.'

The man was full of cheek. She sat.

'I assume you are staying with Rupert,' she said, 'since Cranford marches alongside Glendale, which is where you find yourself now.'

'I am indeed. I didn't have the heart to wake him, for he was dipping rather deep last evening and would not have thanked me for disturbing him. I had no compunction in taking Beau, for Rupert has given him to me to ride during my stay. He's the only horse in his stable large enough to carry me, I'm afraid. I had not expected to lose my way, but the country around here is very beautiful and I ventured further than I had intended.'

'Perhaps it is time then to send you safely home.'

'If you would but point me in the right direction, I shall regretfully relieve you of my company.'

'You are not rid of me yet. Walk with me to the edge of the wood. It will be easier from there to describe the way.'

As they walked, Phoebe learned that Duncan Armstrong had become acquainted with her friend at university. Over the years they had seen little of each other, for the Scotsman had spent much time travelling abroad. He was, he said, a keen collector, and Phoebe found herself envying his ability to go where he would. As much as she loved her home, she had always longed to travel and asked him to tell her something of his time on the Continent.

'Most of it was spent in Italy. One could spend half a lifetime there and see only a small part of its treasures. I intend to return when I have the opportunity.'

'How lucky you were that the troubles were over. With Napoleon safely in St Helena these past three years, it has again become possible to move freely.'

'Yes, and fortunate that my brother did not have the same desire to travel and I was able to leave our home in his capable hands. And now I have filled it with the fruits of my journey and must return soon to put all in order.'

'Your collection is extensive then?'

'Extremely — and because of its nature requires a lot of space.' She looked at him, a question in her face. 'It is mostly comprised of statues, though I was fortunate indeed to pick up a few outstanding paintings.'

Phoebe mentioned to him the Long Gallery at Glendale and he begged to be allowed to visit. 'It is not always the artefacts themselves but the stories behind them that are of significance. I shall have so much sorting to do when I get home. Are there any interesting tales to tell in your own collection?'

'Naturally we have the obligatory ghost.'

'You do?'

'Indeed, though I have never seen him. However, the story has been handed down over the generations — I daresay much embellished, but the essence of it is true I am sure.'

'Splendid. Does your ghost roam the house, or is he confined to the one room?'

'You are making game of me, but I assure you he has been seen. Just not by me. He 'lives' in the Long Gallery.'

'I cannot wait to meet him!'

'We should be delighted to show you our treasures. My father is very proud of them and would, I know, value your opinion. Not of the ghost, naturally; but we have what I believe to be some very fine pieces. Ah, here we are. If you take that track, you will come eventually to the road. Cranford lies to the other side. A small stream runs parallel if

Beau needs water.'

He took her hand and looked down into her eyes, suddenly serious. 'I hope we shall meet again very soon. I shall make it my business to see that we do.'

Then he was gone, and Phoebe was left with a strange feeling in the pit of her stomach that she had never before experienced. Unable to identify what it meant, she shrugged it off and led Jester back to the stable yard. As she entered the house, she found a letter lying on a salver in the hall. The envelope was addressed in her aunt's hand, and she took it with her to her room to read when she had changed out of her riding habit.

She sat at the dresser expecting to see only news in the aftermath of the wedding and any *on dits* that might be circulating in town. She was less than pleased therefore to find that her Aunt Sophia was finding the weather in London far too brutal and proposed visiting the country for a few weeks' respite. *You may expect me within a sennight*, Phoebe read, and with a sigh she went to break the news to her father.

2

Duncan did indeed stop by the stream to slake his own thirst and that of his horse. They walked on slowly, as much because the man was in contemplative mood as on account of the heat. He would have recognised the feeling that Phoebe had experienced in her stomach, for he had also been strongly affected by their meeting. Unlike Phoebe, though, he knew he had met his fate. She was a feisty one and he was by no means sure she even liked him on such short acquaintance. He resolved to get to know her better.

'She might be married,' he said to Beau, 'but she made no mention of a husband. Only of her father. Not that that's by any means conclusive. I found it refreshing, though, to have a conversation with a woman without having to bury my chin in my neck to see down to her face.' He quickened his pace, anxious now to glean as much information as he could from his friend.

Rupert found him in the stable some while later where, having removed Beau's tack, he was in the process of brushing him down and seeing to his comfort. 'They told me you'd been riding. I can only assume it is your bulk that allows you to consume so much wine with such little effect. I, on the other hand, am suffering. Yes suffering, Duncan; and I blame you entirely — challenging me in that way when you knew I would be unable to resist.'

'Nonsense. There were enough times when we were up at Oxford when you drank me under the table. How was I to know you had become soft in the intervening years?' Duncan said, laughing and slapping his friend on the shoulder.

'Ouch. Go easy, man. I have not yet fully recovered.'

'Hair of the dog?'

'No, I thank you. But I will bear you

company while you breakfast. My father has long ago eaten and is out visiting his tenants.'

'First I must change. I am drenched with sweat and must clean up before I do anything else. Do you fancy a swim in the lake?'

'Are you mad? The water is ice cold even at this time of the year.'

'You should try some of the lochs in Scotland. You would know then how cold water really can be. I have broken ice before now. But if you are not keen, perhaps we might visit your neighbour. I would welcome the opportunity of saying thank you, for Miss Marcham rescued me this morning.'

'Oh she's home, is she? And how was Phoebe of assistance to you?'

'I was lost; strayed further than I should and found myself not on your land but on hers. She was good enough to direct me to Cranford.'

'Well I should like to see her above all things. I have sorely missed her company.'

Duncan was perturbed at his friend's reaction. He sounded eager indeed. Was Rupert then before him?

*   *   *

It was some two hours later when the friends drove the short distance to Glendale in the gig, Duncan having changed and eaten his fill. They strode into the house via a door at the back, Rupert being used to treating the place as his own. His companion felt a little uncomfortable, this being his first visit, but had to be reassured by his friend's judgement: 'It is all right and tight. I have been running free here since I was in short coats.' Phoebe was nonetheless startled when they came upon her in the hall where she and Mrs Wiggins were discussing household.

'Rupert! You gave me such a fright. Could you not at least have made some noise as you approached?'

Duncan was encouraged. Her tone to her neighbour was not in the least lover-like. Nor indeed was Rupert's when he responded, 'Well I'm sorry but you must have been concentrating very hard, for we did not creep in for sure. You look like you've seen a ghost.'

'We have had enough talk of ghosts for one day, have we not?' she said, turning to Duncan as Mrs Wiggins withdrew. 'I did not look to see you again so soon, Mr Armstrong.'

He could not judge if she was pleased to see him. 'We have come at a bad time, I can tell. You are busy with your housekeeper and must wish us in Jericho.'

Phoebe was surprised to find him so observant and said so. 'I'm sorry I gave you that impression and it is not the case. It is just that I returned to the house to find a letter from my aunt. She is to descend upon us within the week for what I envisage will be an extended stay. There is much to do, but it can wait. I apprehend you are anxious to see the room of which I spoke?'

'I am, but not just now. I came only

to thank you again and to pay my respects to your father.'

'Come on then, old man. He'll be in his library for sure. I'll take you there now.'

The two men left the hall and Phoebe went again to find Mrs Wiggins to discuss accommodation for her aunt and her cousin Lydia, who was to accompany her mama. Phoebe was fond of her cousin, whose features and temperament strongly reminded her of her own mother, but she could have wished her aunt elsewhere. With her housewifely duties out of the way, Phoebe went in search of her father, for it could not be anticipated that Aunt Sophia was coming to Glendale merely to rusticate. She would expect to be entertained, and she knew the forthcoming visit would sorely tax Papa. She found Sir Edward alone in the library, Rupert and Duncan having left a short while before.

'Nice young man is Armstrong. I like the cut of his jib. No airs and graces about him. I told him he could come and eat his mutton with me any time.'

'That's all very well, Papa, but we shall have Aunt Sophia upon us soon and there is much to be done. We will have to hold a dinner party and a soirée or two. Yes, I know,' she said, a delightful grin transforming her features. 'It is not what you would wish, but it won't be so bad. Lydia will be persuaded by her mother to sing and play the harp.' Here she actually chuckled, for her father's face told its own story. 'You must not blame the poor girl. With my aunt it is sometimes more comfortable to submit than to cross her will, but I do not envy my cousin. She is quite retiring until she knows one well, I believe, and I can only imagine how mortified she will feel if asked to perform in front of strangers.'

'Well I ain't a stranger, and I have no intention of encouraging her.'

'You will not be required to do so, for her mother will be before you. It isn't the evenings I am concerned about, but what we are to do during the daytime if this heat continues. We could have a picnic in one of the clearings in the home wood, or perhaps by the lake in the shade of the willow trees,' Phoebe said, warming to her theme. 'Riding will be out of the question, both on account of the weather and because Lydia has no fondness for horses. Sadly she is afraid of them. Perhaps a carriage ride would suit her, but would my aunt like it?' Edward grunted. Phoebe sighed. 'I know. So much to do. I shall not break your head any longer, just my own, but I thought I should warn you of what lies ahead.'

'I suppose you will do as you must. I wonder how long Armstrong remains at Cranford. He seems an amiable enough fellow and could prove helpful in the entertainment of our guests.'

'Papa, you are abominable!' Phoebe said, a smile chasing the frown from her face. 'The poor man has come to stay with his friend and you are preparing to engage him in order not to exert yourself. You are without shame.' But there was an appreciative gleam in her eye as she left him to his own devices and went to make a list of the various distractions she might arrange for their guests.

★   ★   ★

'You will forgive me, I hope, for calling at such an unseasonable hour, but Beau was anxious to see Jester again,' Duncan said the next morning with an engaging smile. 'I thought you might be repeating your early start of yesterday. But I see you are not dressed for riding. The poor lad must wait for another time. I will leave you to get on.'

'No, don't. It would be heartless of me to dash his anticipation. You could not be more welcome, for I have been torn between my duties here and my desire to be out. You are just the excuse I need,' Phoebe said, smiling. 'If you would but give me ten minutes to change . . . perhaps you will oblige me by asking Will to have Jester saddled and ready. You know the way. We do not stand upon ceremony here.'

★ ★ ★

'Do you need an excuse to take your horse out?' Duncan asked twenty minutes later when to his surprise they were mounted and on their way, he having placed little reliance on Phoebe being ready as quickly as she had promised.

'Only to ease my conscience. Normally I am free to do as I please, but my aunt's impending visit has laid a burden upon me. But I should not be speaking so. You must think me very ungracious.'

'Good heavens, no,' he said, laughing loudly. 'Nothing was ever truer said than one may choose one's friends but is apt to be saddled with one's relatives. I avoid them as much as I can.'

'Do you not then rub along with your

brother and your mother, whom I believe you said lives there too? I am excessively fond of Papa. Indeed I prefer his company to that of most other men.'

'Well that's put me in my place, hasn't it?'

'What? No. I didn't mean that. You know I didn't.'

'I was just teasing. Now let us draw a truce, for we have reached the woods and I think it only fair to give these two their rein.'

No more was said for a while as they cantered along the bridle track, coming to a halt at the same time as if from an unseen signal between them. Phoebe drew her brows together in a frown and Duncan asked immediately if something was amiss.

'Only that my conscience is bearing down upon me. I fear I must return to the house. I have many invitations to write and none to help me. Are you staying long with Rupert, do you know?'

'Are you asking me to help you address the task? My hand is appalling, I must tell you. Even I cannot sometimes read what I have written.'

'Heavens no, I wouldn't presume as much. I was just wondering if I might include you on my list.'

'I am fixed in Somerset for a while and would be delighted to accept any invitation you might be kind enough to bestow upon me.'

'Don't commit yourself so easily,' Phoebe said with a ready smile. 'You are chosen because my father has taken a liking to you. I have no hesitation in telling you that he finds my aunt too busy. She wears him out. Your dual role will be to draw her attention from him and also provide conversation that will be more to his liking.'

'I will do whatever I can to lighten your burden,' Duncan said, serious again and causing her to wonder why she should find his remark so reassuring. She professed that she must return to Glendale and left him to make his own way back to Cranford, reflecting that within two days she had come to regard Duncan Armstrong as a man one could turn to in times of difficulty. She would be sad indeed when he removed himself from the neighbour-hood.

3

The next few days flew by. Duncan's help proved to be invaluable, and he was always ready to place himself at her disposal. To Mrs Wiggins he proved an ally, insisting on one occasion of relieving her of the tea tray. 'Allow me to take this to the master. I know you have much to do and I would speak to him anyway.' Mrs Wiggins was not above taking advantage of his good nature. Since her mistress's demise, there had been little entertaining at Glendale and the servants were being stretched beyond what they were used to. She was glad to accept any small gesture when that nice Mr Armstrong stepped into the breach. Nor was she blind.

Phoebe and Duncan rode every morning before the work of the day began, and six days after receiving her aunt's letter all was in readiness. They spoke often during their daily rides of Armstrong's travels, he entertaining her with tales of conversations in broken Italian and of the time an innkeeper had tried to gull him into accepting inferior accommodation. 'I soon put him to rights.' But mostly her eyes would light up when he talked about the paintings he'd seen, the fine glass he'd found in Venice and the marbles that would forever remind him of Rome.

'Now that all is prepared I think it is time to show you the Long Gallery, unless Mrs Wiggins has given you some commission or other and you have already seen it.'

'Even had she done so, I would have refused to oblige her. This was something you and I had agreed upon at our first meeting and I would not forego that for anything.'

He was so disarming that Phoebe felt she had known him for months, rather than barely a week. She was as at ease in his company as she was in Rupert's. It would be prudent, she knew, to maintain a certain distance, but she found it impossible to do so, so well did his cheerful manner match her own. Who knew, though, when he might be once more off upon his adventures. She would miss him, of that she was well aware, for it wasn't in her nature to delude herself. Well she would just have to face the situation when it arose.

'Then let us go now before we are called upon to do something else.'

Phoebe gasped as she entered the gallery, for in spite of the intense heat outside it felt icy cold. She looked at Duncan, and it was evident from his expression that he was experiencing the same sensation, one dark heavy brow raised in question.

'I have been here many times, but never before have I felt his presence so strongly.'

'It would seem your ancestor is trying to tell us something.'

'You believe that?'

'There are many unexplained things in this world, and to dismiss them out of hand would be foolish. Come,' he said, taking one of hers, 'let us walk the length of the room and see if anything happens.'

Phoebe chose to disregard the effect his touch had upon her and would indeed have been reluctant to withdraw her hand from his. The iciness dissipated a little, but returned with full force as they came abreast of a statue said to be of Simon Marcham and his lost love. The couple were entwined in what was all too obviously a loving embrace. Phoebe found she was gripping Duncan's hand rather tightly.

'Allow me to introduce you to my great great great . . . I know not how many greats . . . grandfather.'

'The family ghost?'

'The very same.'

'Perhaps now might be the time for you to tell me his story but first let us adjourn to another room.'

Phoebe was happy to do so. She had

never before felt uncomfortable with Simon's ghost, but today's experience had taken on a whole new dimension. She did not feel it right to talk about her ancestor in front of him. *Whatever am I saying?* she thought, but there was the realisation that she had always been convinced there was some truth in the story, blasé though she might seem to be.

'So you see, there was no way they would be allowed to marry. There was conflict between their families and they were torn apart. It was Simon who found her lying under a tree in the home wood, or so the story goes. He was inconsolable and for many years became reclusive. Eventually, realising it was his duty to continue the family name, he married without love and produced an heir. Lucky he did, or I would not be standing before you today,' Phoebe said, trying to lighten the tone. Duncan, though, was still looking serious.

'Poor man. No wonder it is so cold in

there. His soul is not at rest.'

'And it is said it never will be until his secret is discovered.'

'What secret is that?'

'That's the trouble. Nobody knows.'

'Then we must make it our business to find out, for he is in torment.'

Phoebe could only be amazed that this huge bulk of a man held so sensitive a spirit. Most would have ridiculed such a suggestion, and so she told him.

'I have handled many pieces of antiquity. Some are cold to the touch; and some, even though carved from stone, have a warmth when one's hand is laid upon them. I did not touch Simon's statue today. I wanted first to hear his story. Forgive me for being presumptuous, but do you hold any records that might give us a clue?'

'There are a few accounts; people's experiences of encountering Simon in the gallery, records of the date he withdrew from the world and again when he emerged from seclusion.'

'I would see them if I may.'

Phoebe, realising there was in this man a genuine desire to help, told him she would fetch them immediately, for they were sitting in her mother's withdrawing room. It had an airiness about it, the mahogany doors a good deal lighter than the oak to be found in much of the rest of the house. The fretwork motif of the doors was replicated around four hand-painted panels that adorned the walls. It was an altogether feminine room, and even after all these years Phoebe could feel her mother's presence there. Her father could no longer bring himself to enter, as it reminded him too acutely of his loss, but for Phoebe it was a sanctuary.

It seemed Emily had been intrigued by the tale and insisted she had several times encountered Simon's ghost. She had gathered what information she could, and it was stored now in a chest within a flat fronted mahogany sideboard that stood beneath his portrait. Phoebe had just placed the chest on the table when the sound of horses was heard through the open window.

'Oh no, it is my aunt! Isn't it just like her to come at this moment!'

Duncan smiled. 'I think perhaps we can excuse her for not knowing how bad is her timing. May I take this with me back to Cranford?'

'Forgive me, no. I would not have it leave the house. You are welcome any time to look at its contents with me, for I too cannot wait to study them. Drat the woman; it would seem that waiting is exactly what I shall have to do.'

Duncan slipped away through the back of the house, promising to come back next morning for their customary ride and assuring Phoebe that should she feel the need of his support, she need only send a message and he could be with her in no time.

* * *

'Aunt Sophia, how lovely to see you again so soon,' Phoebe said with a calm she was far from feeling. 'And Lydia. Did you travel well? For I know it is a tedious journey.'

'Very well indeed. James is aware of my problem and took great care.'

Her mother looked pityingly at her as she handed a grossly over-decorated hat to the footman, whose face was so wooden that Phoebe was hard put not to smile. Baroness Talbot, a robust woman, had never suffered any degree of sickness when travelling and had little sympathy for her daughter, feeling certain she could overcome her affliction if only she would try. Phoebe was far more compassionate and suggested her cousin might like to be shown to her room to recover.

'I would indeed, Phoebe,' Lydia said, smiling ruefully. 'Would that I could accustom myself, but long distances always leave me burned out, and no amount of resolution overcomes the problem.'

'And you, Aunt Sophia — would you care to retire for a while?'

'No, I thank you. I shall first see Edward.'

Phoebe summoned the footman to escort her aunt and accompanied Lydia to her room. She knew she should have diverted her aunt, but for the moment her cousin's needs were greater. By the time the younger girl had removed her bonnet and her luggage had been deposited she was in a good way to being recovered.

'I can't think why it is, Phoebe, and I know Mama has no patience with me. I have always enjoyed walking; any outdoor recreation. It is the motion that defeats me.'

Lydia looked up into her cousin's expressive brown eyes, her own startlingly blue ones brimming with tears.

'Don't distress yourself. You are fagged to death. What you need is a period of repose and you will be in much better frame in no time. I will draw the curtains, for I cannot imagine this bright sunlight is helping.'

'You are right. I have a headache and

feel you must think me a very poor creature.'

'Not at all,' she said, looking over her shoulder as she pulled the drapes together. 'I shall leave you now and return in plenty of time to take you to supper.'

Phoebe did not think Lydia a poor creature. She could readily believe that hours spent in a coach with her aunt would be enough to exhaust even the sturdiest of creatures. She closed the door gently behind her, certain that her cousin would be asleep before she reached her father's library. Pausing outside her father's sanctum for just long enough to set her features in a welcoming smile, Phoebe entered the room. It was immediately evident that he was not well pleased, although fortunately Aunt Sophia was not well enough acquainted with him to realise.

'Ah, Phoebe. I trust my niece is settled. Be good enough to escort your aunt to the drawing room. I shall join you shortly when I have finished my business here.'

Nothing could have been more affable than his tone, but the glint in his eye warned that he would deal with her later. *Oh dear*, she thought, *and so soon after my aunt's arrival.* As for him joining them shortly, she placed little reliance on the statement. It would be left to Phoebe to entertain her aunt for the rest of the afternoon.

The drawing room to which Edward had referred was not her mother's room, no more than her father would Phoebe invite her to that private area. The place that was customarily used for entertaining was quite a dark room, the colour on the old panelling having further deepened with the passage of years. Sophia, however, was impressed, for to her it declared the heritage of the old house. She had only once before visited Glendale. Her sister, aware of her husband's antipathy both to Sophia Talbot and her now deceased husband, had not issued more than the one invitation. It was Emily who had travelled to London in times gone by. Phoebe too had visited the capital during her first Season; and her aunt, to her credit, had generously but unsuccessfully tried to see her established. It was not an experience she had wished to repeat, and her father made no push to insist she did so.

'I admit I was astonished to find how grown you were when you came to us for Clarissa's wedding, though of course it had been six years since last I'd seen you,' her aunt said.

'But Aunt Sophia, I have been this tall for many years,' Phoebe replied innocently, her wayward sense of humour unable to resist teasing. The lady understandably appeared irritated.

'You misunderstand me. I meant that the inexperienced girl I knew had become a mature young woman. Have you no thought to your future? You must be deemed to be almost beyond making a good match.'

'My future is my concern, ma'am,' she replied tersely, for she would brook no interference. 'Would you like me to have some tea brought in before I show you to your room? It is evident that my father has been detained.'

'No, thank you. Perhaps it is time I went to see how Lydia is getting on,' Sophia said, rising and judging it prudent to ignore what she felt was disrespect from her niece, for nothing was more certain than that she had been dismissed.

'I suspect she is still fast asleep. Allow me to escort you to your chamber. I shall see you are called in time for supper.'

Not wishing to exacerbate an already tense situation, Sophia had little choice than to comply, but Phoebe was biting her lip. While her aunt was a guest at Glendale, it was ill-mannered indeed to have antagonised her, no matter the provocation. *We are at loggerheads already and she hasn't been in the house above an hour yet. However are we going to rub along for several weeks?*

* * *

Supper was not quite the ordeal Phoebe had anticipated. Edward had recovered his humour, Lydia her spirit, and Sophia was evidently determined to exert herself to be nice (in her niece's opinion condescending) to everyone. The plans for her entertainment were made known to her and she expressed appreciation, not having expected, she said, that they would put themselves out to such a degree.

'Invitations have not yet been despatched, for we did not know exactly when to expect you, but I shall see that they are delivered in the morning. Unless our immediate neighbours are free and can be persuaded to join us, we shall dine quietly tomorrow. Thereafter, I hope you will find there is sufficient to amuse you during your stay.'

'You are too kind, my dear. Lydia and I thought only to escape the heat of the city. We did not anticipate you would go to so much trouble on our behalf.'

'Would you prefer the solicitations remain unsent?' Phoebe asked, wide-eyed and innocent, but she would not meet her father's eye.

'No, no. Now that your proposals are in place, it would be a pity to forego them.'

4

'It was fortunate that you weren't present, for I should certainly have given myself away, but I so wished you'd been there to enjoy the joke.'

Phoebe and Duncan were sitting again on the fallen tree where they had first met. He had thought her a little overwrought in the stable yard, but after a good canter she was as relaxed as ever in his company and smiling now as she related what had happened the previous evening.

'Does she always rub you up the wrong way?'

'Almost invariably. But when I stayed with her in London, I was able to hold my tongue. I was her guest, and it would have been unforgivably rude of me not to. Here at Glendale, I will not have her cutting up my father's peace. It seems to me that if I can inject some humour into the situation, be she never so aware, I am able to restrain myself.'

'Is her understanding so inferior then?'

'By no means. She is intelligent enough. Just that she has no sense of the ridiculous. I cannot believe how unalike she is to my mother, who could make anyone laugh by merely a word or even a gesture.'

'I wish I could have met her. I have a less than warm relationship with my own mother and never experienced the joy that is so obvious when you speak of yours.'

Phoebe looked searchingly at him, for it seemed he had become sad. He answered the question in her eyes. 'She preferred my brother and was never at pains to hide it.'

'Oh, I'm so sorry!'

As they walked the horses back, Phoebe invited him for supper that evening together with Rupert and his father.

'We are to act as peacekeepers?'

'Is that how it seems? I fear you are right and that subconsciously it was my intention. Nonetheless, I would be delighted for myself if you could join us. It seems to me we have not yet shared a meal, and I cannot remember the last time Rupert and Max dined with us.'

'I shall accept your invitation gladly and will pass it on to the others. Do you have a difficult day ahead of you?'

'No, for Lydia is a delight and reminds me so much of my mother. I need only escort my aunt about the house and show her one or two of our more grand possessions and she will be most affable.'

'Sets a lot of store by that sort of thing, does she?'

Phoebe went on to tease him about his own collection and to ask if he too set store by it. He countered by assuring her that he regarded each piece not as a possession but as a treasure of which he had the privilege to be the guardian. They parted company as they exited the wood, but their anticipation of the evening to come left them both in high spirits.

★　★　★

'We are invited — you, Max and I — to dine at Glendale this evening. You may know that Baroness Talbot and her daughter arrived yesterday.'

Rupert laughed. 'I'd like to see Sir Edward do the pretty at a formal occasion. More likely to excuse himself and disappear into his library. As for Phoebe, well, she don't much like to stand on ceremony either. You know what; I think maybe we should stay at home and enjoy a quiet game of piquet. I've just remembered what she told me about the aunt. A bit of a harridan, she said. Yes, definitely a game of piquet.'

Duncan was having none of it. 'Where is your chivalry, man? Miss Marcham needs you.'

'No, you go. That will do the trick. I shall play with my father.' But Max, when the proposition was put to him, was all for visiting his friend. The fact that Edward employed a very fine chef might also have had some influence on his decision. Rupert gave in with good grace and the two younger men went off to try their hand at fishing.

* * *

Phoebe found her aunt and cousin in the drawing room. Sir Edward was nowhere to be seen. She was determined to be on her best behaviour.

'Forgive me, aunt, for I have this moment returned from my morning ride. I do hope you have not been waiting long.'

Sophia, for her part just as determined to be genial, assured her they had themselves only just arrived. 'I took some hot chocolate in my bedchamber earlier and that served me for a while. Certainly I was in no way ready to rush about in this heat. Not that it isn't much pleasanter here than in London, for although it is hot, it is not stuffy.'

'And are you quite recovered, Lydia?'

'Indeed I am. I slept so soundly that I knew nothing until my maid drew back the curtains.'

Phoebe suggested they might, armed each with a parasol, take a walk about the gardens. She assured them there were several tree-shaded benches where they might sit and admire the view, promising later, when it became too hot, to return to the house when she might show them one or two of the rooms they had not yet visited.

'Glendale is so vast one might surely spend months and still not see all its chambers,' Sophia said. Phoebe blanched at the thought. However, her proposal met with approval.

* * *

'Good heavens! Is that you, Wiggins? I thought you must have retired years ago.'

'Well, Miss Sophy,' the housekeeper

replied, using her nursery name and reducing Baroness Talbot to a child again, 'you are out there. You will see that I am still on my feet and certainly not ready to give up yet.' Phoebe, remembering that Mrs Wiggins had acted as nursemaid to both sisters, was astonished to see the effect she had on her aunt. For the first time ever she found her quite endearing. Doubtless it wouldn't last, but it was refreshing to see.

'And this is Miss Lydia. Well, you are so like your Aunt Emily I should have known you anywhere.'

After this exchange of greetings, the ladies enjoyed a light luncheon before beginning their exploration of the house. Phoebe chose to take them to the Long Gallery. One or two land-scapes hung there, but it was mostly given over to statuary. She hadn't been since going with Duncan and was curious to know how palpable her ancestor's presence would be. There was no rush of cold air. Phoebe had to conclude that Simon Marcham was particular about whom he showed himself to. She was slightly disappointed, feeling that her aunt would have been truly impressed to encounter a spirit from another time. Then she remembered what Duncan had said about a soul in torment, and she felt only sadness. Lydia was delighted with a painting depicting the exact scene they had admired when seated on a bench in the garden, though Phoebe didn't consider it to be one of the artist's finer works. The rest of the day went well; and with a promise to see on another day the room that held some fine examples of porcelain, as well as that which housed the greater part of the art collection, they retired to their rooms to prepare for the evening.

★　★　★

Even in the small dining room, and with seven at the table, it felt overly large for the number of people assembled. Sophia found no fault, though, much preferring the grandeur of this room to that of the small parlour where Phoebe and her father normally enjoyed their meals together. They were waited upon by several members of staff, the lady of the house keen to impress her aunt in any way she could. Phoebe placed no store by such pomp; but if that was what her aunt was expecting, then that was what she would find.

One thing became very obvious before the evening was much advanced. Rupert, normally garrulous in the extreme, was very quiet and could hardly tear his eyes from Lydia. A well brought up young lady — for her mother was only too aware of how harmful it could be if one was deemed to be fast — Lydia, having once caught Rupert's gaze, blushed charmingly and looked away. Thereafter she did not look at him again, but concentrated her attention upon Sir Edward on one side and Duncan on the other. Poor Rupert had to be content with chatting to Phoebe on the one hand and conversing with Sophia, to whom he had taken an instant dislike, on the other. However, he quickly realised that if he were to have any chance of advancing himself in the eyes of the daughter, he would need the mother's approval. He could be charming when he chose, and on this occasion he chose.

Sir Edward was able to talk to Max, who sat on his other side, and was therefore able to consider that the evening had gone off well. 'Very well indeed, in fact,' he told his daughter in an aside when the ladies left the gentlemen to their port.

$\star$ $\star$ $\star$

Phoebe had little opportunity to talk to Duncan, and the evening was considerably advanced before they had time for a few quiet words.

'I hope I have done as you wished.'

Phoebe didn't pretend to misunderstand. Duncan had engaged Lydia in conversation and facilitated an exchange between Edward and Max. Her father was content and her aunt was impressed.

'I am grateful indeed. I was astonished to see Rupert so taken with my cousin. My only experience has been as a pseudo-sister; but his small attentions after supper — bringing her fan, putting her shawl about her shoulders when it turned cooler — showed him to be a man of no little charm.'

'Whereas I had so little opportunity I could not even engage you in conversation.'

Phoebe looked up at him. His gaze was serious. She could not misunderstand, but was too unsure of her own heart to encourage him in this vein. Instead she said, 'Simon made no appearance this afternoon when I escorted my aunt and cousin to the Long Gallery. I wondered if he is receptive only to sympathetic visitors, and am more anxious than ever to examine the contents of my mother's chest. It would be unfair, though, to do so without you, for I feel he spoke to us both the other day. I shall do what I can to create an opportunity. How to be rid of my aunt for a couple of hours is the thing.'

'I'm honoured that you choose to include me,' he said formally; and then, much more in character, 'I would be most put out if you did not, for everything indicates that this must be a shared adventure.'

'Perhaps we may contrive something between us. Will you ride again in the morning?'

'Of course. It is the best part of the day.'

'Then we will have the freedom to discuss it further.'

Phoebe bade him goodnight and went to bed wondering if the adventure he referred to was that of Simon, or if he was alluding to something else even closer to home.

★   ★   ★

'I cannot believe it! Max has invited my aunt and cousin to take tea at Cranford this afternoon, though I am sure it was at Rupert's instigation the invitation was extended.'

'Undoubtedly, for Rupert has spoken of nothing but the fair Lydia since we left Glendale last evening. Her clear blue eyes. Her straw-coloured hair. How appealing is her reticence.'

Phoebe smiled delightedly, for this was not behaviour she had ever observed in her childhood friend, nor had she suspected him capable of it. 'Our butler must have put something strong in his wine to make him talk so.'

'Certainly he was behaving as if intoxicated — but not, I think, from the wine.'

They talked more of the projected tea party, Phoebe saying that even her father had consented to go. 'I think because he is hoping for an opportunity to discuss with Max the merits of a horse in his stable that Papa is tempted to buy.'

'Does he still ride then?'

'No, this would be a carriage horse. He still enjoys tooling his gig about the estate.'

'And are you too going to Cranford this afternoon?'

'That is just what's so convenient. I may send my apologies and we can instead investigate the chest in my mother's drawing room. Unless, that is, you are obliged to be present.'

Duncan assured her it would be an easy matter to make his excuses and that he would ride over to join her later.

5

Phoebe was in a fever of excitement for the rest of the day, and honest enough to acknowledge that it wasn't only the prospect of their research that was the cause. The ladies strolled again in the garden, Lydia delighting in the maze and challenging her cousin to find the exit before her.

'How can you be sure I do not know its secret?'

'That would be too bad! Do you?'

'No, for I haven't ventured in there since I was a child and have never found my way out without help.'

Phoebe summoned a footman to sit in a high chair overlooking the labyrinth and the girls were guided to the centre. Each was determined she would be first to find the exit. It was cool enough in the shelter of the hedges, if a little airless. In the end neither resolved the mystery, and abandoned the search when Sophia was heard calling from outside. They were guided out and joined Lydia's mama on the bench, where she was waiting for them.

'I see you have had a fine time. It has been very pleasant here, but now I should wish for some refreshment; for even with the parasol I am becoming uncomfortable.' It was said without rancour; she was in good spirits, and Phoebe began to hope her stay at Glendale would not be quite as taxing as she had anticipated.

Time passed quietly enough until the party was ready to set out for Cranford. They talked of Clarissa's wedding. Sophia commented that the visit to Glendale was a godsend. She had been so busy for so long, what with all the shopping and the dressmaking and a hundred and one other things besides, that it was a relief to be still for a change.

'Though I enjoyed it immensely and would be happy to do the whole all over again,' she said, looking pointedly at her daughter and causing her to blush.

Phoebe was impatient for them to leave, but she contained her frustration well enough. Sophia and Lydia went to retrieve their bonnets while Phoebe made sure her father was ready. When they asked why she wasn't joining them, she said there was much she had to do at home and she would see them later. Having waved them off, she went straight to her mother's withdrawing room, retrieved the chest and set it on the table. Then she sat down to wait for Duncan. He didn't keep her waiting long. He strode into the house through the back with no more ceremony than Rupert would have shown and entered the room just as she was ordering some tea.

'Good afternoon, Mr Armstrong. Would you care for some refreshment?' she asked, barely able to contain her excitement in front of the footman. He asked for a tankard of ale and sat beside her.

'Perhaps we should wait until the footman returns with the tray.' Not even to herself did she sound convincing.

'When I consider how I rushed over here, riding poor Beau far harder than I should in this heat, I am astonished you can even ask me such a question. Come on, girl. Get on with it,' he said, eyes brimming with laughter.

She ignored the appellation but could not help responding to the man's charm. She'd never met anyone like him before; and though no slave to convention herself, she was nonetheless amazed at how disregarding he was of its boundaries. Her recent attendance at Clarissa's wedding had only confirmed that she was destined for spinsterhood. She didn't enjoy life in the capital; and since she knew every gentleman of marriageable age in the vicinity of Glendale, the likelihood that she would meet her fate was small indeed.

It had nonetheless come, in the form of a giant of a man with few airs and graces but with whom she had felt an almost instant bond. Phoebe had to acknowledge that she had tumbled head over ears in love. In just a few days he had stolen her heart. But who was to say he wouldn't disappear as quickly as he had come?

Duncan watched as she drew the chest towards her and opened the lid. It was a sizeable container and full to the top with documents. The uppermost was in her mother's hand, and it was plain she had meticulously catalogued every item. They began at the top of the list, not wanting in their eagerness to get things out of order. After examining the first few, Duncan remarked that every single one contained some reference or alluded to Simon.

'It would seem that she was entirely focused on him.'

'Yes; I always knew she had a deep interest, but this is way beyond what I imagined.'

Some time went by. The footman came and went; and though everything held their interest, there was no clue in the documents they uncovered as to the family legend. Several different hands had penned what they had read, so it seemed Emily wasn't the only person who had taken an acute interest in the tale. Phoebe had taken a clean sheet of paper and copied her mother's list, item by item. She didn't want to deface what Emily had prepared, but desired a record of her own that she could annotate.

They came to a notation that said merely 'poem'. Phoebe added it to her list and took the next piece from the chest, and she gasped.

'I feel it too,' Duncan said. 'Simon is here. Is he asking us not to look, or wanting us to go ahead, do you think?'

'I truly believe he wants us to see. Look, it is in his hand. He has signed it at the bottom. Shall I read it aloud?'

'Please.'

Simon would a wooing go, his true love for to see

They met in secret, no-one knew,
  and carved their names upon a
  tree
Cruel fate took her away from
  him and left him all alone
But they are bound forever now
  immortalised in stone

If you would choose to venture
  and to find the place of tryst
Known only to the two of them,
  the place where first they kissed
Then take the cup into your hand
  and drink down to the base
There will you find the clue to
  guide you surely to that place

Simon Marcham

'This is it, Mr Armstrong. This is the clue. Oh, poor Simon. And his love, whose name we do not even know.' She paused a moment, looking around. 'He's gone, hasn't he? Now that we have found this, he has gone. He knows we will pursue it.'

'But your mother had this before us, and maybe others too. None has yet solved the riddle,' Duncan said as gently as he could.

'Then we shall be the ones to do so,' she said with all her usual spirit. 'But which cup was he referring to, and how are we ever to find out?'

*   *   *

Rupert was furious with his father, as much as a man of his mild temperament could be. And with Edward too, for the pair had gone off to inspect the horse and left him to the tender mercies of Lydia and her mother. While he was delighted to have a chance to spend time with Lydia, there was no way he could speak as freely as he would have liked; he was not insensitive to the rigid back and forbidding demeanour of her mama. Rupert made it his aim to bring her onto his side.

'I trust you are enjoying your stay at Glendale, ma'am. There is much to interest one, is there not?'

'It is an elegant home and one I much admire.' There was no softening in Sophia's expression. No fool, she had observed his interest in Lydia. A mere country gentleman would not do at all. She had other plans for her daughter.

'We had such fun this morning,' Lydia said far more enthusiastically. 'Phoebe and I spent an age in the maze, neither of us able to find our way out.'

Rupert laughed. 'It was one of our favourite games as children, for you must know that we played together all the time, neither of us having siblings and our places lying so close together.'

It was evident from her raised eyebrow that the baroness did not approve. Rupert had spoken in all innocence, but he had obviously offended Sophia's sensibilities. He tried again.

'I am vastly looking forward to the soirée they are holding this evening. It is to be hoped you will not think it flat after those you must have attended in London.'

'I *never* make comparisons between London and the country.'

She wasn't making it easy for him. Rupert was searching around trying to think of what to say next when Sophia said, 'I am disappointed not to see your friend here today, Mr Armstrong is it?'

'He asked me to make his apologies, ma'am. Said there was much he had to do and was anticipating the pleasure of seeing you again later.' It wasn't the truth, but he felt there was no harm in trying to placate this obviously difficult woman.

'Miss Marcham said as much when we left the house.'

'Did she? I dare say they are together then.' The words were out before he could stop them and regretted immediately. The eyebrow was raised even further; the back more rigid than ever. Rupert then unintentionally made the situation worse, saying, 'They are great friends, you know. They ride together every morning before breakfast, for both are horse mad, and it gets far too uncomfortable later in the day.'

'I doubt her groom appreciates having to go out so early.'

Rupert laughed. 'Phoebe take her groom! I'd like to see him try.'

'Are you saying she rides with Mr Armstrong *unaccompanied?*'

Oh dear, that's upset the apple cart, Rupert thought. He was never so glad as when Max and Edward chose that moment to return. Sadly, though, the damage was done.

* * *

'You know, Father, I always thought Phoebe was exaggerating about her aunt but between you and me she has severely understated the case. The woman is a shrew if ever I met one,' Rupert confided after the visitors had departed. 'She took me in dislike straight away, that's for certain. Well that's spiked my guns for sure. You will have noticed how charming Lydia is. I have had no opportunity to fix my interest with her, and now I shall be lucky if the woman lets me within ten feet of her.'

Rupert ran his fingers through his hair in frustration. His relationship with his father was quite open, and he had no hesitation in laying open his feelings to Max who would be, and indeed was, the first person he would turn to for help.

'Of course I have noticed, and I am happy to see your regard light upon such a personable young lady. Whatever else the mother might be, she has done well with her daughter.'

'It's not just that. She'll be after Phoebe now, and Duncan too I dare say, for I foolishly told her they went riding unchaperoned. You should have seen her face when I dropped that into the conversation. Well honestly! On her own land. And in any case, she's past the age of marriage, so what harm can it do?'

His father smiled.

★ ★ ★

The evening was not an unqualified success. Phoebe was astonished when her aunt swept into the house with a far from convivial expression, for she had thought they'd parted company on good terms. Nothing was said, however, and each retired to their rooms to prepare for the evening's entertainment. Phoebe had engaged three musicians to play for her guests, though none was better received than Lydia, who, gaining command over her nerves, performed very sweetly, accompanying herself on the pianoforte to the satisfaction of all.

To those local gentry and dignitaries whom Phoebe had seen fit to invite to her soirée, Baroness Talbot was condescending in the extreme. No-one found anything amiss in her manner, for it was what they might have expected from one who lived in *London*. To the Marchams and the visitors from Cranford, she was, however, so distant that Phoebe remarked to Duncan in a quiet moment that she thought Simon had drifted into the room, so cold did she feel. Rupert was sulky as a bear, for he could get nowhere near Lydia; Lydia was embarrassed by her mother's behaviour, and Phoebe was at a loss to know what was wrong. Edward and Max ignored everyone and enjoyed a quiet conversation together. Only Duncan, observing all, had a thoroughly enjoyable evening, for his sense of humour was brought to bear. The food that Phoebe's chef had so carefully prepared turned to ashes in her mouth, and she retired at the end of the evening wondering why she had so put herself out for someone who so little appreciated it.

★ ★ ★

'Are you lost to all sense of propriety?' Sophia asked her niece when she returned from her morning exercise.

'To be riding with a man unaccompanied! Whatever would your mother have said had she been alive today to see you?'

'She would most certainly have joined us, for she was as fond of riding as I am.' Phoebe was just managing to control her temper.

Sophia spluttered, 'That my child should be witness to such activity!'

'Oh but she wasn't, dearest aunt, for she was still in her bed.'

'You deliberately misunderstand me! I blame your father, who has allowed you free rein to the extent that you have forgotten what is expected of a young lady.'

While it was unlikely that Phoebe would brook criticism of herself, it was absolutely certain that she would not do so on her parent's behalf. Unable to restrain her anger any longer, she said, 'It is not I who forgets herself, ma'am. While you are in my father's house, you will speak of him with respect!'

'I fear I can no longer remain. Have

my carriage summoned immediately. I shall take my leave of you.' With which comment Baroness Talbot swept majestically out of the room, or such at least was her intention. Unfortunately, she tripped over the hem of her gown and fell awkwardly. An ominous crack was heard. It seemed she would not be leaving quite yet after all.

6

Several people appeared on the scene, for Sophia's cries of pain were loud and long. First to reach her was Phoebe, who was nearest to hand. With a glance she could see what had happened and was overcome with remorse, for she was as sure the accident wouldn't have happened had she spoken in a more level way. Someone was sent immediately to summon the doctor. Sir Edward, seeing his daughter had control of the situation, stepped back in the library and closed the door. Mrs Wiggins appeared and dropped to her knees beside the patient.

'There there, my sweet. Be a brave girl, for I shall not leave you. The doctor will come soon and make you comfortable again.'

'Oh Wiggins, it hurts so,' said Sophia, her face pale, her eyes frightened; but the wailing stopped. Her old nurse would look after her. Baroness Talbot, a child once more, gave herself gratefully into the other's care before thankfully swooning away.

Fortunately Lydia, walking with her maid, did not return to the house before the doctor arrived and her mama had been carried back into the drawing room and placed tenderly upon a chaise longue. Everyone but Mrs Wiggins was banned until he had set the ankle. 'Fortunately it is a clean break and should heal with no problem. I shall prescribe some laudanum for the patient, but she must be kept quiet. On no account are you to attempt to carry her upstairs to her chamber. She must not put any weight upon that foot.'

'No, sir,' said Mrs Wiggins. 'I shall see to it that a bed is set up for her in this room, and someone will be with her at all times.'

'Very well. I know you for a sensible woman and will ensure she is comfortably situated. I shall return tomorrow to see how she goes on. In the meantime, as soon as she awakes, try if you will to get her to take the medicine. I have a small amount in my bag but will bring a further supply early in the morning. Good day to you.'

As the doctor was leaving, Lydia entered the house to be greeted by Phoebe who, while carrying the burden of guilt, was sensible enough to realise that punishing herself would in no way help her aunt.

'You must not worry, Lydia, for she will be well, but your mother has met with an accident. I will take you to her now. She is in the drawing room, and there she must remain, for she has broken her ankle.'

The doctor, hearing what was said, was satisfied that there were at least two practical women to minister to his patient. Nor did the daughter look to be the sort who would have hysterics.

★   ★   ★

Phoebe scribbled a hurried but detailed note to Duncan.

. . . and now I am filled with remorse; for I know, had I not let loose my wretched temper, it would never have happened. So you see, I shall be unable to ride with you tomorrow morning — not on account of what my aunt has said, but because duty dictates I must be here when the doctor arrives, and I know not when that might be. Yours, PM

Duncan chuckled, for he read far more into it than was on the page. Having no other commitments that afternoon, he rode over to Glendale to sympathise and perhaps, if he could, to lighten her burden.

They went to her mother's drawing room, for it was an opportunity to look at the papers again. 'You must know you made me laugh aloud this morning,' he said. 'Poor Miss Marcham. In one moment you had thought you would be rid of your unwelcome guest, and in the next her stay was to be protracted beyond what you had ever thought.' He smiled in a way that made her realise how well he understood.

'Was it very bad of me? I was so pulled down, but I can see now there is some humour in the situation if I but look hard enough.'

'But it wasn't as bad of you as you are making out. You are human, after all. How does she go along now?'

'Lydia sits with her, which is why I am able to have this time with you, for I could not otherwise leave my cousin alone. But the greatest blessing is Mrs Wiggins, who has taken complete control of the sick room. She has embraced her old charge. I don't know if you're aware that Mrs Wiggins used to be nurse to my aunt and my mother? Baroness Talbot has slept most of the time since the doctor left this morning. Moving her onto the bed that has been made up in that room was an ordeal which I think has taxed her strength, and in any case I believe the laudanum will have made her drowsy.'

A frown marred her features for a moment, causing Duncan to ask what else was amiss. She explained that having accorded so much effort for her aunt's entertainment, all would now have to be cancelled.

'But why? There is still Lydia to think of; and while her old nurse is taking care of her, she cannot expect your cousin to sit around all day and every evening.'

One quizzical expression let him know that Phoebe thought she could expect just that.

'Surely,' he said roguishly, 'she can trust her daughter to your chaperonage.'

This caused Phoebe to laugh, for her humour was never far beneath the surface. Duncan was satisfied, remarking that with nothing fixed in the calendar for that day they were able to relax and, if the doctor came in good time in the morning, the projected picnic could go ahead.

'And it will be so much more pleasant without my aunt to frown upon us all.'

'I fear you are unjust. I have had some conversation with her and found she possesses a keen sense of humour.'

'Maybe you are right, but it hasn't been much in evidence where I am concerned.'

*   *   *

An hour went by in a flash, but Phoebe and Duncan were no nearer to solving the riddle of the poem, nor did the rest of the papers reveal any further information other than historical. They sent for some tea and reviewed what they had so far uncovered.

'I used to love riddles as a child, but I am frustrated beyond saying by this one. My mother must have spent years trying to uncover its secret.'

'And possibly many others have done the same,' Duncan reminded her gently, for he could feel her disappointment. 'We have only just begun our search. From her collection, it would seem your mother spent much of her life here at hers. It is plain the poem will not give up its solution easily.'

'Well, Great Great Great and many more Greats Grandpapa,' Phoebe said, turning to the wall and raising her cup to his painting, 'I salute you, for you have baffled many generations.'

Duncan too turned, holding his cup before him, but hesitated in the act of taking a sip, spluttering and causing the liquid to drench his cravat with a soft brown stain. He smiled broadly. 'Have you ever noticed, Miss Marcham, that in this portrait Simon is holding a goblet?'

His excitement was palpable, and her eyes flew again to the image of her ancestor.

'Do you recognise it? Do you know where we might find it?'

'Of course I do. It will be in the room where all the silver is kept. Come,' she said, jumping up, 'let us go there at once.'

Phoebe almost ran to the door but pulled up short as it opened in front of her, the edge catching her cheekbone as she jumped away. Lydia, stumbling into her, was filled with contrition and offered to fetch a wet cloth to hold against her face.

'Allow me,' Duncan said. 'You may tell your cousin how your mother does while I am gone.'

He returned a few minutes later, his fingers touching Phoebe's as he passed the pad to her. She was covered in confusion, and he was hardly less affected, but Lydia was turned away and happily did not notice.

'Thank you,' Phoebe said in a voice strangely unlike her own.

'Hold it there as hard as you can against the bruise. You may that way avoid some swelling,' he said tenderly.

'I am so sorry. I was just coming to tell you that my mother awoke for a few minutes but is sleeping again now.

Mrs Wiggins insisted I take a break, for she could tell I was distressed. It is so unlike Mama to be submissive, you see; yet she obeys everything Mrs Wiggins says to her. I had to ask if perhaps she had not damaged her head as well.'

Duncan reassured her, saying that if she was feeling pulled it was more than likely that she would give herself over to the ministrations of her old nurse. Phoebe looked at him from under her lashes but thought it kind of him not to make game of Lydia.

'Mr Armstrong was just leaving,' she said, thinking she ought to give some time to comforting and entertaining her cousin. Impossible in any case now to begin their search. 'We shall look forward to seeing you and Rupert tomorrow at noon.'

'The picnic goes ahead then?' Lydia asked.

'As long as the doctor has been and gives consent to leave your mama with her nurse. Will that suit you, sir?'

'We shall be certain to be here at the allotted time.'

Phoebe said she would send a note should a problem occur, and would do likewise to the squire, whose two girls were to join the party. It was to be hoped it would not be necessary. Duncan left and Phoebe, still clutching the pad to her face, looked again at Simon Marcham's portrait. Could they be right? Was this the clue that would lead them to the solution of the riddle?

* * *

The doctor was as good as his word, arriving just as the family were finishing breakfast. Phoebe persuaded Lydia to remain with her father while she went to see her aunt, 'for you will only be distressed, you know, if he has cause to pull her about somewhat.' Such was not the case though. Satisfied that there was nothing more to be done at present, the doctor took his leave, promising to call in a week's time to check on his patient. Phoebe took her aunt's hand and said in all honesty, 'I would not have had this occur for all the world, Aunt Sophia. Please forgive me. Had I not distressed you, this might never have happened!'

Baroness Talbot, though she could be a difficult woman, was not an unreasonable one. 'We perhaps both said things we now regret. Let us put it behind us and make the best we can of the situation. I look to you to entertain Lydia during my infirmity and trust you will see to it that she is suitably safeguarded,' she added in a more robust manner. *Well*, thought Phoebe, *she offers me a straw, and it is comforting to know at the same time that she has not lost her spirit.*

* * *

The day being marginally cooler, the picnic went ahead to the enjoyment of all who attended. Thomas Wainwright escorted his sisters, Mary and Elizabeth, having returned only the previous day from visiting friends in Brighton. Phoebe was surprised to see Max; and Sir Edward, persuaded by his daughter to attend, was delighted to have his friend to bear him company. She was mindful that suitable chaperonage should be provided. One glance at Duncan convinced her that he had encouraged Max to attend for the same reason; and when she quizzed him about it later, he admitted it to be the case, 'for I had not thought you would be able to bring Sir Edward up to scratch.'

'I agree he is as impatient of convention as I am, but he knows his duty. In any case,' she said with a smile that reached her eyes and his heart, 'he knew his sister-in-law was not here and was thus perfectly ready to join the party.'

Cooler it may have been, but to have exposed oneself to full sun would have been foolhardy. Phoebe had planned the picnic well, choosing to go the short distance to the lake rather than subject Lydia to a carriage ride that might make her feel unwell. A clump of willow trees threw shade upon the grass, and blankets were laid beneath them. Chairs and a table had been carried from the house as well as two large picnic baskets. A third was added by the gentlemen from Cranford, and various additions had been brought from the Squire's home.

'Mama insisted, you being kind enough to invite us, that we made some contribution,' Elizabeth had said.

Thomas, his holiday in Brighton still fresh in his mind, chose to pull off his coat and boots and dangle his feet in the water. Attempting to stand, he discovered very quickly that the ground sloped away at a sharp angle, and he found himself out of his depth and overbalanced. He spluttered to the surface full of merriment, declared it to be a great lark, and submerged himself once more. Naturally Rupert and

Duncan thought it tremendous sport and followed him in, Rupert forgetting his aversion to cold water.

The young ladies retreated from the water's edge, none wishing to be splashed; but when Thomas emerged, he embraced each of his sisters, causing Mary to exclaim that he was the greatest beast in nature. It was all in good fun and, with an appetite that only the young seem to have, the various meats, cheeses, pies and other delicacies were consumed with an eagerness which, had the kitchen staff of the various establishments been able to see, would have given them much pleasure.

Rupert, hoping for an opportunity to become better acquainted with Lydia, was not gratified that she gave as much attention to Thomas as himself. It didn't occur to him that there was no way she would show preference for one man over another even if she felt it — which, truth to tell, she did. He would have been thankful to learn that from their first meeting she had felt drawn to him. Thomas Wainwright, though likeable enough, was just a boy. Rupert, older and more sophisticated in her eyes at least, seemed the epitome of the hero in one of the books from the lending library that she was so fond of reading.

'Fine chaperons Edward and Max have turned out to be,' Duncan whispered to Phoebe, pointing to where both men were dozing gently.

'I'm certain their presence is not really required. Even my aunt would surely see that, with this number of people assembled, no harm could come to my cousin.'

'One would hope so at least. I'm not sure who has had the best time — the two of them; the young ladies; Thomas, who entertained us all so well with his antics in the water; or Rupert, who followed him in.'

'An action you did not hesitate to emulate.'

'It was too good an opportunity to miss.'

'At least you all had the foresight to remove your coats and boots. Are your clothes yet dry?' It was not for her to add that the sight of him, his wet shirt clinging to his muscled frame, had evoked in her feelings she preferred not to acknowledge.

'Thank you, yes. And now that I have been able to spend some moments with you in private conversation, I can answer my own question.'

'Which question was that?'

'The one as to who has had the best time. Undoubtedly it was I.'

Phoebe, who had bent to brush some grass from the hem of her gown, looked up quickly into his eyes. They were steady and serious. She said nothing, for what *could* she say?

7

Mrs Wiggins laid aside the book she had been reading aloud to Baroness Talbot. 'Like the girl within these pages, your daughter is a credit to her mama. A very prettily behaved young lady she is. You've done a good job there, Miss Sophy.'

Her defences down, her trusted confidante at hand, Sophia opened her heart. 'It has been hard, Wiggins. Unlike my sister, I did not marry for love. Only you knew how entirely my heart was given to another. Deemed by my parents to be unsuitable, it was my duty as the elder daughter to form an alliance that met with Papa's approval. I struggled to keep up appearances for many years, but in truth I have never been as happy as since Talbot passed away.' These last words were spoken with an almost apologetic smile. 'I thank heaven that Clarissa has married the man of her own choosing, and my ambition for Lydia is that she will do the same. But how can I be sure she will make the right choice?'

'Tell me why you are looking so worried. Is there someone? A person of whom you disapprove?'

Sophia went on to explain. Two very flattering offers had been forthcoming, but when she had approached her daughter, it was found that her feelings were not engaged.

'Then both suitors shall be rejected, I told her, but I could see she had thought I might coerce her into marriage with one or other. It may not appear so, Wiggins, but we are very close, and I am happy to say that Lydia confides in me. To the outside world, I know I appear to be a very managing person; but I believe this to be the product of my circumstances.'

Mrs Wiggins turned away to pour some water for her patient, but in truth it was so she would not see the tears that had sprung to her eyes. The happy young girl had grown to be a lonely woman who had erected a protective wall about herself.

'Lydia is still very young, miss. Are you afeared her fancy will light upon someone you think unsuitable? Even I have noticed Mr Brendon is quite particular in his attentions.'

'Is anyone ever worthy of one's daughter? No, I do not worry on that account. He is a personable young man, but is he the right man for Lydia? I would see her well-established.'

'By well-established, do you to mean financially well-established?' Mrs Wiggins asked. Sophia acknowledged the question with a guilty nod. Her nurse pointed out that Lydia's idea of comfort might not ride with her own. The Brendons were a traditional family, fixed in Somerset for generations, even though their name did not carry a title. 'Do not make the mistake your parents made. It is possible, for she is an obliging girl, that Lydia might marry to

94

accommodate you, for I am sure you have not told her of your own circumstances.'

Sophia's expression arrested. Mrs Wiggins was satisfied and left her patient to mull over what had been said.

★   ★   ★

The picnic party split up in due course, but they resolved to do it again soon. Phoebe and Lydia went straight to the drawing room, but as Sophia was fast asleep, they retired instead to their own bedrooms. Lydia sat on the bed with every intention of passing the next hour absorbed within the pages of a book. As she read, the hero, of whom she had not previously formed a clear vision, appeared to her in the guise of Rupert Brendon. The words swam before her as she relived every moment spent with him that day. Did he like her? Had he given her any greater attention than Mary and Elizabeth? She could not tell;

for Rupert, like herself, had been raised to observe certain niceties. Had he a preference, he would not, in public at least, have allowed it to show. *And there is no chance I will see him in private,* Lydia thought, blushing at the very idea.

★ ★ ★

Phoebe's impatience did not allow her to stay long in her chamber. Full of guilt (for she considered this to be Duncan's adventure also), she entered the room containing the family silver. Her excitement mounted; she was certain she would soon hold in her hands the solution to Simon's riddle. She had assured Duncan she knew of the location of the goblet. Not that she had ever seen it, but because aside from the ugly epergne that graced the table in the main dining room and other pieces placed for ornamentation, the rest of the collection was to be found in this place. Phoebe began a systematic search at one end of the room. It was exhaustive, but some long while later she had to admit defeat. *I cannot have missed it*, she thought, not wishing to repeat the whole process. *I will have to wait for Mr Armstrong's help after all, though I have been meticulous and do not now believe the goblet is here.*

It was a quieter than usual Phoebe who sat down to dine with Sir Edward. Lydia was taking her meal with her mother in the drawing room, and it was the first time for days that father and daughter had been alone.

'You are looking disturbed, Phoebe. Do you have something on your mind?'

'Not at all,' she replied, not wanting to burden him; not knowing either if he had been aware of her mother's fruitless search. She didn't wish to rake it up, for even at this distance her father was sensitive to his loss. 'I was reflecting upon today's activities. It went well, don't you think?'

'Splendidly. Max and I were able to indulge ourselves in just the way we like. We have arranged to go fishing tomorrow — that is, if you haven't organised some other treat you wish me to participate in,' he said, looking at her with a jaundiced eye.

'You are free to go to the trout stream, for nothing is to happen until the evening. You will recall that we were invited to the Fairweathers'. I sent my apologies, naturally, explaining about my aunt's indisposition, but they begged we still attend, and my cousin with us. I asked Aunt Sophia myself, but she insisted we go and is happy to have Mrs Wiggins sit with her for the evening. I believe she is finding it a comfort to have responsibility removed for a while. She worked hard during the approach to Clarissa's wedding.'

'Are you finding it a burden, entertaining your cousin?'

'Not at all. She is a delightful girl. Tomorrow I plan to take her to Bath, for it is no great distance if we take the Wolverton Road. We were discussing the London shops, and I informed her of the several superior establishments to be found in Milsom Street.'

Sir Edward wondered that they would undertake such an expedition. He knew of Lydia's dislike of travelling.

'This cannot compare with the journey from Eaton Square. It was Lydia's own suggestion that we go.'

'In that case, I shall enjoy my fishing without the feeling that I have not given you adequate support.'

'And perhaps, if you are returned before us, you might spend a while with my aunt,' she teased. Both laughed, and for the time being at least, Phoebe was able to put the riddle of the goblet aside.

* * *

Phoebe and Duncan, enjoying their habitual ride the next morning, stopped in the clearing as usual. The weather was cooling so as to be almost pleasant out in the open, and Duncan confided that he was looking forward to going fishing with Max and Edward, he and Rupert having been invited to join them. Phoebe told him of her intention to journey to Bath with her cousin, 'but we shall be back in time to see you at the Fairweathers'.'

'Yes, it seems we shall have to put off our search for another day.'

Phoebe didn't pretend to misunderstand him, and confessed to having been a little disappointed beforehand, 'but to no avail, for it is not there.'

'I have not yet been in the room; but if it is anything to compare with others in your home, it must be like searching for a needle in a haystack.'

She laughed and admitted it to be somewhat cavernous. 'But I feel sure I should have found it, had it been there. I have racked my brain to no avail trying to think where else it might be.'

'And it is not the sort of establishment one could search from top to bottom. We could be old and grey and still not have discovered its whereabouts,' he said, smiling ruefully.

'To be truthful, I doubt if I have even seen the whole myself. I cannot understand what possesses people to build homes they are never going to be able to fill.'

'To outdo the neighbours of course,' he said with a laugh.

It was decided they should search the silver room together at the next opportunity. Parting at the exit to the wood, Duncan went back to Cranford and Phoebe went to change into attire more suitable for a day's shopping than one in the saddle.

* * *

Lydia was in fine spirits and professed when they reached Bath that she felt as fresh as a daisy. As they had been sitting all the while, Phoebe suggested they might first take a walk in Sydney Gardens and perhaps venture into the Labyrinth, so much had they enjoyed themselves in the home maze.

'Well if you are not famished after

that, I certainly am,' Phoebe said as they retraced their steps along Great Pulteney Street. 'Shopping must wait until we have refreshed ourselves, don't you think?'

'Yes; I am excessively thirsty. Should we partake of the waters? I have heard they are very beneficial.'

'And very distasteful, I assure you. We shall instead visit Sally Lunn's Tearoom. I trust you are enjoying your visit to Glendale. Such a pity your mama is so incapacitated; you must be tied in the country perhaps for longer than you would wish.'

Lydia assured her cousin it was no such thing; and that truth to tell, she envied Phoebe her rural existence.

'Well I have to say it would not be my choice to reside in a large city, but you have lived in London all your life! There must be all manner of things there to entertain you.'

It was acknowledged to be so, but the oppression in the summer and the mad round of events at other times Lydia found absolutely exhausting. She had not enjoyed her coming-out Season; and though the theatre was exciting, one did not go every day, after all. In company her reticence was taken for shyness, 'and I fear I must appear somewhat insipid to those with whom I am not acquainted.'

'Never say so!' Phoebe exclaimed, though she had at first acquaintance also imagined her cousin to be painfully shy. 'Does your mama know of your sentiments?'

'No. Though we are close, I would not burden her, for I can see no way my situation will alter.'

'Upon your marriage, perhaps?'

Lydia seemed for a moment to be covered in confusion. 'You will not know that I refused two very eligible offers. But I could not bring myself to accept either, as my feelings were not engaged. Mama exerted no pressure upon me, and yet I am aware she must be disappointed. And now the thought of returning to London fills me with dread. I know I shall be expected to participate in all those things I find most distasteful.'

Phoebe folded her hands and regarded her cousin thoughtfully. She had observed Lydia and Rupert. There was no doubt in her own mind that they were strongly drawn to one another. If Lydia did indeed desire a life in the country, nothing could be better. What, though, of her mother? No wonder the young girl was feeling despondent. For the moment, nothing could be done, so Phoebe had recourse to something that over the ages had given cause to uplift the spirits.

'Come — it is time to go shopping.'

8

Fifteen sat down to dine that evening. Fortune was not on Lydia's side. Thoughtful hostess that she was, Harriet Fairweather was aware that to place Thomas Wainwright next to either of his sisters would not be welcome. Max was seated next to the vicar's wife, a lively and talkative lady whose company would always be enjoyed. Phoebe sat by Squire Wainwright, 'and I must apologise: I know he is profoundly deaf, but you are one of the few people I can rely upon to ensure he does not feel isolated,' their hostess confided at the first opportunity. Thus, Lydia and Phoebe had of necessity to ignore Rupert and Duncan, who were across the table from them; Mary, Elizabeth, Edward, the squire's wife and the vicar making up the rest. Lydia was well entertained by Thomas, and Phoebe was adept at diverting the squire; but both women were glad when the meal came to an end and the ladies adjourned to the drawing room to be joined by the gentlemen after they had drunk their port.

Duncan, no slave to circumspection, made straight for Phoebe's side, taking the chair next to hers.

'I trust you enjoyed the fishing. Were you successful?'

'Yes, and threw some back, for we cannot consume them all.'

'Perhaps I mistake the matter, but could it be that you bring the scent of fish with you?' she said, smiling, for she knew he would appreciate her teasing him.

'No such thing, for I went from stream to lake and had a good swim, removing I am sure any residual odour.'

Dismissing the vision this conjured up, she was for once grateful when asked to perform on the pianoforte. No relief was to be had there, however.

Duncan followed her to the instrument to turn the pages for her and was the first to congratulate her on the fine singing voice that had accompanied her playing.

'Is there no end to your talents?' he said.

'You make too much of it, sir,' she replied crisply. Her aptitude, though adequate, was not above the ordinary.

'No, you are supposed to say 'Thank you' while at the same time bowing your head modestly.'

She laughed aloud and he with her, causing the rest to ask what was the joke. Duncan handled it well enough, but there could be no doubt now in Phoebe's mind that he was wooing her. She spent the rest of the evening trying to ignore him, but succeeded only in smiling at the most inappropriate moments when he caught her eye, well aware of her discomfiture and, drat the man, enjoying it.

★ ★ ★

Lydia was gratified when Rupert engaged her in conversation.

'It was kind of your mother to allow you to join us this evening,' he said. 'I trust she is not in too much pain.'

'No, indeed. I fear it is the incapacity that frustrates her, for she is such a doing woman. Were it not for Mrs Wiggins, I think she would be bored past reason.'

'Mrs Wiggins?' He knew her, of course, having run freely through Glendale since childhood, but was unaware of the former connection.

'She was my mother's nurse before coming to Glendale upon my aunt's marriage. It is fortunate their relationship is such that I am able with confidence to leave Mama in her care.'

'Phoebe tells me she has been showing you some of the delights of Bath today. I trust you were not too uncomfortable. It is still very warm.'

Lydia was touched that he seemed so concerned for her welfare and hastened to reassure him. She even told him of the yellow ribbon she had purchased to adorn one of her bonnets, before then apologising for boring him with matters inconsequential.

'Not at all. I look forward to seeing the results of your stitchery; I am sure it will look delightful.' He glanced a moment over his shoulder. 'I wonder, Miss Talbot, if you would like to take a turn about the garden. The doors are open, and we shall all the time be in sight of the rest.'

There seemed no good reason for refusing to accompany Rupert to the terrace, and they spent a while in silence admiring the view and delighting in the companionable silence.

* * *

Edward leaned against the cushions and fell asleep as the carriage took them back to Glendale.

'Perhaps you can see now what I meant earlier today. In the country everyone is so relaxed. Nobody displays any airs and graces or puts themselves forward to impress.'

Phoebe smiled, thinking that Rupert had very much set out to impress. Naturally she did not say so to Lydia.

'Yes, a delightful evening. I am truly fortunate with my neighbours and my friends. I hope you are pleased with what I have arranged for tomorrow. Mr Armstrong and Mr Brendon have invited us to for a picnic lunch in the grounds of Cranford, and I have accepted on your behalf as well as my own.'

Her cousin looked shocked until Phoebe told her that naturally her abigail would accompany them, 'and it will be no hardship to her, I know, for I am fairly certain she has her eye on the second footman.'

'Then of course I shall be delighted. But what of Mama?'

'I'm sure she will not object; there is little you can do for her for the time being. However, on the spur of the moment I invited the two gentlemen, together with Mr Max Brendon, to spend a quiet evening with us tomorrow. My father shall be persuaded to join us,' she said, glancing in his direction as he breathed in noisily. 'And if your mother is happy to recline on the chaise longue, we will sit with her in the drawing room.'

'How very kind of you, Phoebe. I am sure she must by now be craving company, though she never complains.'

Surely this cannot be the same woman who arrived at Glendale little more than a week ago, Phoebe reflected, though she was tactful enough not share the thought with her cousin. 'Papa,' she said, placing her hand on her father's arm and nudging him gently, 'we are home. It is time to rouse yourself.'

Sir Edward looked a little sheepish. 'Very good evening. Nice to meet up with old friends.'

Which made Phoebe laugh, because her father was not the most sociable of men. It would seem that the Talbots' visit was doing a lot of good in more ways than one.

* * *

Some hours later, Phoebe awoke from a disturbed sleep. She had dreamed that Duncan was riding away from her, and as fast as Jester galloped, Beau was quicker. 'Wait!' she had called out in her dream. 'Wait — we have not finished our mission!'

But horse and rider disappeared over the horizon, and she woke up. She was shivering, thinking it was because of her dream; but then came to the realisation that Simon's spirit was in the room with her. This was only the second time he had made his presence known other than in the Long Gallery. She felt strongly that he was trying to tell her something and that there was a connection between her dream and his being here. 'I shall not give up, Simon. I promise you,' she said aloud, at the same time sensible to the fact that she was talking to thin air. Or was she? As she finished speaking, the iciness left the room. She lay down again and fell for the rest of the night into an untroubled sleep.

★ ★ ★

The next day dawned bright as ever but more comfortable, for there had been a storm during the night that had left a freshness in the air. When Duncan met Phoebe in the stable yard, he remarked that Beau was dancing on his toes and ready for a good gallop. 'And I am glad of it,' he said. 'The horses must have been feeling the heat as much as we. Shall we give them their heads?'

She nodded her assent, and they were off.

'You are looking very fine this morning,' Duncan remarked later when they had reined in and settled into a walk. Phoebe could not help but be pleased, for her new riding habit had only yesterday arrived from London and naturally she had to wear it at the first opportunity. 'The blue contrasts well with your hair. I particularly like the military cap and its plume of feathers.'

'I see you are an expert on such matters,' she said, choosing to ignore the personal nature of his remark.

'Not at all, but I know what I like when I see it.'

Phoebe did not relay her dream to Duncan, not being at all sure as to its meaning, but she told him of Simon's 'visit'. 'I wonder does his spirit feel that we are getting closer to the solution.'

'I don't know, but I assured him I wouldn't rest until we have resolved it. The strange thing was that after I had spoken he disappeared again, hopefully confident of our tenacity.'

They were by this time almost out of the woods. 'Lydia and I will join you in a while, but I must first spend some time with my aunt. I fear I have been sadly inattentive.'

'It is to be hoped you can recover

ground later. I shall do my very best to entertain her this evening.'

'I am depending on you,' she said, smiling as she took her leave of him.

★ ★ ★

'Aunt Sophia, I hope you will not pluck crow with me, for you must be feeling sorely neglected,' Phoebe said with an apologetic smile when she entered the drawing room.

'Not at all, my dear. I have not until now been looking for company. Wiggins has supplied all my needs and it is truly only in the past twenty-four hours that I have been feeling the fidgets.'

'You are uncomfortable?' Phoebe asked, dismayed.

Her aunt laughed. 'No indeed. Merely desirous of joining society again. You must know that the doctor has been already this morning and given me permission to exert myself a little. I am greatly anticipating this evening; Lydia tells me you have arranged something for my entertainment.'

'Just a very few friends to bear us company, but I hope it will suffice to amuse you. I am so sorry I was not here when the doctor came.'

'It is of no matter. I have received the reassurance I needed. He seems to be a good man, and I trust what he has told me. I confess though to feeling a little tired after his call, and will spend some time resting while you join your neighbours for a picnic. I will see you later.'

Phoebe could almost have believed her aunt had undergone a change of personality, so gracious was she. Leaving the room, she went herself to fetch her bonnet and to find her cousin.

★ ★ ★

Phoebe was, she felt, old enough to be alone with a man without drawing reproach upon herself, in spite of what her aunt might think. But Lydia must

116

of necessity observe society's mores. Consequently, Phoebe felt more like a maiden aunt than a cousin, as she ensured that Rupert and Lydia were not left unattended during their time at Cranford. However, Duncan suggested they might all take advantage of the kinder conditions and go for a walk. Lydia and Rupert walked in front and her maid followed behind. Phoebe and Duncan fell even further back, thus allowing the others to have private conversation. It was perfectly innocuous.

'Your mother is improving, I hear.'

'Yes, and greatly looking forward to your company this evening.'

'I am glad of the opportunity to further my acquaintance with her. And perhaps to alleviate her boredom, for I cannot believe she is not by now in need of diversion,' Rupert said with a smile.

'She said as much to me this morning, though I think she has no immediate wish to return to town. But she is a sociable creature and never happier than when in the company of others.'

'Your stay at Glendale must of necessity be prolonged. Forgive me when I say I am pleased it should be so.'

Lydia didn't know how to answer, so she looked at him with a smile, stumbled and would have fallen had he not caught her arm. A flush appeared in her cheeks, she thanked him, and they walked on.

Rupert was a man who had always been up for a lark, and his friends would have been astonished to learn that from the moment of meeting Miss Talbot he had desired nothing more than to be able to take care of her and shield her from harm. He was frustrated that for the present at least he could be of little service to her. He was not to know that his quiet assurance was just what she liked, and if she thought of Thomas Wainwright at all it was to compare the boy with the man.

Rupert, overwhelmed at first, was content now to take his time. He had never been so happy as when he was with Lydia — nor had he ever been as anxious, for he could not judge whether or not she favoured him above any other.

'My childhood friend is a changed man,' Lydia said. 'Ever since I have known him, he has been primed for any adventure. It is one of the things I liked best in him, but this maturity suits him I think.'

'Allow me to assure you he has not entirely abandoned his previous ways. Only the other day when we went fishing, he grabbed my ankle and attempted to tip me into the water.'

'Now that sounds more like the Rupert I know,' she said, laughing. 'And did he succeed?'

'No. Though he is by no means a small man, I had the greater weight.'

'And dare I ask if you sought revenge?'

'You should not; for had I indeed

done so, it might be deemed I was taking unfair advantage.'

She chuckled again. 'You do not deny it, however.'

'Allow me to tell you that the stream of which we speak is but a short distance from here. Any more of that and were I not a gentleman, it might be that you would find yourself plunged into the water. Just for fun, of course.'

'You wouldn't!'

'Appealing as the thought is, no, I would not.'

9

Nothing could have been more convivial than the group that gathered in the drawing room at Glendale that evening. Though Phoebe had ensured there was sufficient refreshment to satisfy the most demanding of guests, nothing else was put in place for their entertainment. The card table was brought to the side of Baroness Talbot's chaise longue, and she entered enthusiastically into a game of piquet with the elder Mr Brendon. Upon declaring 'I couldn't possibly' when Duncan approached her with the offer of sherry, she was persuaded to take a small glass. He then left them to their obvious enjoyment.

The rest played jackstraws with all the eagerness of children not yet out of the schoolroom, even Sir Edward declaring it great sport. Lydia proved to be the star of the evening, winning several times before Phoebe declared she had finally met her match in a game she had before considered all her own.

'You have rendered me bankrupt, but I promise you I shall come about another time when we sit down to play whist.'

'Clarissa used to declare she would not play with me because I had such a steady hand. Should I have said?' she asked, looking innocently at her cousin but with her eyes brimming with laughter.

There is more to this young lady than meets the eye, thought Duncan. *She is enchanting and will do for Rupert very well.*

* * *

When he told Phoebe of this during their ride the next morning, she replied, 'They seem eminently suited, I agree. But is he not, do you think, a little old for her?'

'I understand there was just such a disparity in the ages of your parents. And yet — forgive me if I speak out of turn — you have given me to understand their marriage was a happy one.'

They parted company soon after, Phoebe relieved to have had her uneasiness laid to rest in the end, as it transpired their paths would not cross for the foreseeable future. When Duncan arrived back at Cranford, Rupert had his foot in the stirrup in the process of mounting his horse.

'I was just about to come in search of you. This man has ridden night and day. Your mother has fallen ill, and there is some doubt as to her survival. She begs you to come.'

'Tell me, lad, how was she when you left?' Duncan asked, turning from Rupert to the courier at his side.

'As to that, sir, I cud na say. Only that the master charged me wi' bringing this letter as fast as I could. Your brother did tell me he had only left his parent's side to place it in my charge and to give me your direction, hoping that you'd still be here.'

'Then we must leave at once. Rupert?'

'Of course. Take Beau and another of my horses; this one has been ridden flat out. You may send them back to me when you change mounts on your way.'

'I am in your debt. Thank heavens I sent word to Fergus of my direction, or he would have had no idea how to contact me. You there,' he said, turning to the lad, 'wait while I pack a saddle bag. Dinna fash yersel,' he added, falling easily into the old familiar dialect. 'I shall not be many minutes. Are you fit to travel so soon?'

The boy looked offended and Duncan took that for a yes. He thought of Phoebe and regretfully dashed off a quick note to her, and then they were off.

'How long did it take you to reach me?' he asked when they slowed to a walk to give the horses some respite.

'Above six days, sir, though I rode as hard as I could.'

'Then we shall try if we can to do it *within* six days. But we must make sure you get a good night's sleep tonight, or I'll be leaving you on the road to recover.'

'You never would, sir.'

'No, though I might be tempted,' Duncan said with the open smile that made so many warm to him.

★ ★ ★

It was a tedious journey and Duncan had much to occupy his mind. At the first stop, he arranged for the return of Rupert's horses. He then made the decision to continue at a slightly less hare-brained pace.

'I shall be of no use to my mother if I collapse upon my arrival,' he told Tom.

They made a good meal and continued on their way, covering much ground before engaging to stay the night at an inn. Duncan lay on his back, his feet hanging over the end of the small bed, his arms folded beneath his neck. Staring up in the dark at the invisible ceiling, he thought of his mother and wondered if he would be in time. He had not been home for a long while. Life had been such an adventure, and now he berated himself for his selfishness. It was true, though, that their relationship was not close, and it was his ties with his brother not his mother that might have prompted him to return sooner.

He turned onto his side and conjured up a picture of the young woman who in little more than two weeks had come to mean so much to him. What would she make of his note? He'd dashed it off so quickly he could scarcely remember what he'd said. Heaven knew when he would see her again, and in the meantime she would have to carry the burden of her aunt's visit alone, as it seemed doubtful that Sir Edward would be of much help. He gave himself a mental shake, for it was not in his personality to worry over what he could not change; and he fell into a fitful sleep.

*   *   *

My dear Miss Marcham, he had written,

I am called home in some haste. Forgive me, but it seems I shall have to abandon you to search alone. Yours regretfully, Duncan Armstrong

He had told Phoebe his hand was indecipherable, but she had no difficulty in reading his short message. It had more of an effect upon her than she liked to admit. What was so urgent that he could not take half an hour to take his leave of her? She couldn't know that his formal address had been deliberate; that he'd thought she would be amused by his oblique reference to Simon, but she had not been privileged to see his rueful smile as he wrote. She had no call upon him. Perhaps she had made more of his friendship than had been offered. What she had taken for something stronger was likely to be merely the open manner of a man with few airs and graces.

Feeling more than a little wounded, she went to tell her father that Mr Armstrong would not after all be joining them for the various planned entertainments. He expressed his regret.

'It seems I shall have to fulfil my obligations to Baroness Talbot without his aid. A pity. I wonder what took him off in such a hurry.'

'It is not for us to question his reasons. Forgive me, Papa. I must go now and consider what further diversions to put in place for my aunt's pleasure.'

Phoebe went to her mother's drawing room and settled down with various pieces of paper. However, her pen made no changes, for she spent some time staring out of the window. Coming to the conclusion that men were not to be relied upon, except for Papa of course, she tried to put Duncan Armstrong out of her mind. It was of no help that she kept visualising his ready smile and recalling his humour, seemingly so well to match her own. She realised too how much his aid had lightened her load. That he would not now continue to do so rendered it heavier than ever, and she could only be grateful for Sophia's seeming change in personality.

Their other venture troubled her even more. It was something they had embraced together, and now she would have to continue alone. And continue she would. She had, after all, given her word to Simon. 'Men!' she exclaimed aloud; and taking her pen in hand, she settled down to the task in front of her.

★   ★   ★

As Duncan headed north, the scenery changed and so did the weather. They rode through thunder and lightning, keeping a firm rein on their horses and driving them forward. Though skittish, they cantered on without bolting and were rewarded, when the storm abated, with a titbit and a 'well done, lad' from both riders.

Duncan rode long and hard in daylight hours and slept soundly during the night. It had been nearly three years since last he'd been home. Fergus understood. It was something to do with being a twin, and he knew why Duncan kept his distance. He felt no joy in being favoured by their mother. But as he rode, Duncan reflected that she was still his mother. Would he be in time? Would there at last be a reconciliation?

Eventually Duncan leapt from the saddle and raced to the entrance of his family home. The door was flung open, and he stood a moment facing his mirror image before being folded in a bear-like grip by his brother.

'How is she, Fergus? Does she still live?'

'She is gravely ill, and it is my belief

she waits only to make her peace with you.'

'As if she cares,' Duncan said bitterly.

'You'd be surprised. She knows how she drove you away. She even asked me to write and beg you to come home, but I knew from your own letters that the wounds cut too deep. But it's time, brother. There can be no excuse for what she did to you, but you are still her son.'

'Though she renounced me!'

'Do not let her take her guilt to the grave. Come, I will take you to her now.'

* * *

'Phoebe. Phoebe!' her cousin repeated in a louder voice when it was evident the other was lost in a daydream.

'What? Oh, I am sorry, Lydia. I was in my mind planning the final details for tomorrow's soirée.'

It was not true, but her reflections were not of the kind she could share with her cousin. In the week he'd been gone, Duncan had intruded upon her thoughts many times. He invaded her dreams as well, and the dream always the same. She was running through a dark passage, Duncan behind her and Simon in front. And then she slipped, fell and lost consciousness.

Morning brought no relief, for she didn't feel rested. Each day she rode Jester but gained little joy from the experience. She stopped as ever in the clearing, trying to remember every moment she had shared there with Duncan. Her horse now was the recipient of her confidences, 'for if I do not talk to someone I shall run mad.'

Phoebe had for the first time in her life fallen deeply in love. She had no idea whether or not her feelings were reciprocated. A stranger to the art of dalliance, she couldn't trust her own instincts. Had Duncan merely been amusing himself? Not unkindly; never that, for she would not believe he might be so cruel. But perhaps it was a game he had thought she would understand. Rupert had by now apprised her of the cause of his sudden flight. Surely, though, had he felt as she did, his note would have contained more than just a reference to Simon.

'I was merely wondering whether I should wear the blue or the yellow muslin to the dance this evening.'

'Dearest, you will look delightful in either,' Phoebe answered, concentrating her attention once more upon her cousin. 'Sadly I am unable myself to wear yellow, for it chases away all the colour in my face. You may wear almost any shade to advantage. Blond hair, blue eyes and such a warm skin tone that complements every hue. Were it in my nature, I would envy you,' she said with a smile.

'But Phoebe, do you not realise how beautiful you are?'

Phoebe laughed. She had never admired her own auburn curls and brown eyes, thinking herself very ordinary. 'Now I know you are trying to gammon me. Wear the yellow then, if you will, and I shall try to achieve some tone by myself wearing blue.'

★ ★ ★

Phoebe, spending the evening with so many friends and neighbours, couldn't help enjoying herself. Harriet Fairweather chose to surround herself with people, and would have done so every day had her long-suffering husband not begged for the occasional respite. 'Which is all very well, my dear, but he takes as much delight as I do in having company.' She had invited only ten couples, 'for I much prefer it when I can speak to everyone present — a proper conversation you understand, rather than a snatched word or two.'

Phoebe was extremely fond of Harriet, who had been a close friend of her mother's and figured largely in her childhood before Emily's demise. And afterwards too, for having no children of her own she had made sure to see her goddaughter regularly. Edward, having withdrawn into himself, was of little help, and Rupert was her only contemporary, though older by three years.

'My cousin has expressed the same opinion. It seems that small gatherings are more to her taste than the large functions she was obliged to attend in London. It is kind of you to include her.'

'Not at all. She is an asset to any occasion.'

It was true. Lydia, in the short time she had been in Somerset, had endeared herself to all. Harriet looked across the room to where Miss Talbot was deep in conversation with Rupert.

'I wonder if they will make a match of it, those two,' she said to Phoebe, whose ready smile reached her eyes in spite of her own situation.

'I hope so. How my aunt will regard such an alliance is another consideration.'

'You think she will not approve?'

'She has but recently lost one of her daughters to matrimony. She may not yet be ready to lose another.'

10

Duncan stood in the doorway to his mother's bedchamber. Visions arose of being taken in her arms as a child, soothed when he grazed his knees, tickled playfully at other times. The images were so strong that it took some moments for them to clear. Behind him, his brother put a hand on his shoulder. He moved towards the bed.

'Fergus, is that you?' Mrs Armstrong asked in a failing voice. Her hand, claw-like, gripped his.

'No, Mama. It is Duncan.'

The grip tightened and she turned her head to see him better. 'You have come!' she whispered. 'At last you have come.'

He sat beside her, his throat constricted. 'Do not tax yourself, Mama. I shall not leave you.'

Tears crept from the corners of her

eyes and onto the pillow. 'I have written. Ask Fergus to show you.' But she did not release his hand. Duncan looked at his brother.

'She was frightened in case you didn't come; in case you came too late. It was some weeks ago. I had not expected her still to survive,' he said in a voice too low for his mother to hear. 'Here,' he said, handing Duncan a sheet of paper. The windows were covered against the dwindling daylight. He struggled to read, an unaccustomed mistiness in his eyes impairing his vision. He recognised his brother's hand, but it was his mother's voice that spoke in his head.

I pray that God will forgive me, for I will understand that you cannot. When your father died, I had no thought for your own loss; only for the man who was my very life. I blamed you for being in the water, when it was I who should have been keeping watch over you. I saw your father dive in; watched him disappear; waited for him to return to the surface, not knowing his foot had been caught amongst the weeds. Instead it was you who bobbed up; you who were saved. The bitterness of my loss turned upon you. I blamed you, you see.

Duncan looked at his brother. 'Did you know of this?'

'Not until Mama charged me with writing it down. I had no more notion than you of the reason for her rejection.'

You cannot know how many years I have regretted what I did — but it was too late. If I could but see you once again, I shall go to my grave in less torment than I have carried for so long.

The brothers knew of course that their mother's antipathy towards Duncan stemmed from the time of their father's death. The change had been immediate. What they hadn't known was that she had considered him to be the cause. But for his brother, Duncan's double loss might have destroyed him entirely; but there was an invisible bond that enabled the one to pull the other through. What Duncan would have done a few weeks earlier might well have been different, but he had 'met' Simon Marchant. He fervently believed now that a soul could exist between two kingdoms in grief and pain. He could not condemn his mother to such a possible existence.

He leaned over and kissed her brow. 'I didn't understand. But I am here now. Rest a while. I will not go away again.'

★   ★   ★

'You were remarkably gentle with Mama. I find it hard to believe you have forgiven her so readily.'

140

'And you would be right to feel so. Knowing the reason will at least stop me wondering, but I cannot purge the pain in so short a time.'

'And yet you did not recriminate.'

Duncan looked at his brother before taking a sip of whisky from the glass he had been nursing between two large hands. They were sitting one at each end of an old oak table in the room that had been the favourite of both as children. The space beneath its surface had in the past served as a fortress, a make-believe battlefield, and even on occasion a hiding place. Tonight they had dined there.

'Had I not returned home, I would have felt no remorse but it would be cruel to reject her now. She seeks a forgiveness I cannot bestow, but she is looking also for peace of mind. If I can help her to that end I will do so, or I would carry a different sort of guilt to my own grave.'

Duncan was looking haggard, and at his brother's suggestion retired to bed, 'for you have had a long and tedious journey. Tomorrow we will talk of other things. A great deal has happened in the three years you have been away.'

'Jane and Malcolm are away from home, I gather. I would hear more about them.'

'And so you shall; but not until tomorrow, when you will hear so much you will be begging me to stop.'

'You the father of a son. I find it hard to believe,' he said, smiling at last.

'Tomorrow, Duncan. Now go to bed.'

★　★　★

It was the day after the soirée. Sophia was resting, having enjoyed the evening immensely but feeling the need to gather her resources again. Lydia had gone to visit the Wainwrights, but Phoebe had declined the invitation, confident she could leave her cousin to the care of the squire's good lady. Though she thought of Duncan every day, she had resigned herself to the fact

142

that she might never see him again. There had been no word, but there could hardly yet have been. In any case, he made no mention of writing to her in his short note.

I must, I shall forget him.

She was in her mother's drawing room and looked up at Simon's portrait. *Did you mean, I wonder, to set us such a difficult task?* He didn't reply.

She moved to Emily's desk and opened the bottom drawer. When she attempted to pull it further, it resisted. Thinking it must be caught on something, she curled her fingers up inside to find the culprit. What she found instead was a catch that caused the drawer to spring towards her. Curious now, she grasped it with both hands and wiggled, whereupon it came away from its housing.

Not entirely surprised, and more excited by the moment, she reached in. Probing with her fingers, she withdrew her hand, which now clasped a silver goblet. *The* silver goblet. There could be no mistaking it. *So, Mama, you succeeded further in your search than we had imagined. How excited Duncan will be when he finds out.* Then she sat back in the chair, saddened because she might never be able to tell him.

She began to examine her treasure. She turned the goblet in her hands, peering at the engraving around its rim, but could find nothing significant. She looked at the underside, but that too revealed nothing. Then she remembered the words of Simon's poem:

Then take the cup into your hand and drink down to the base

There will you find the clue to guide you surely to that place

With trembling fingers, she looked inside. Engraved upon the bottom was the Marcham family crest. She felt elation, and then despair. The goblet had been in her mother's drawer not because she had uncovered its secret but because she hadn't. Glendale was riddled with examples of the family's

144

crest. There was not one single room where it did not appear.

She turned again to the portrait. *You were clever, Simon. Too clever for your descendants, for I don't even know where to begin. Great and many times Great-grandfather, I salute you!*

★ ★ ★

'Do you not think it time, Papa, to put this feud behind you?' Phoebe asked her father when discussing arrangements for the next few days. 'We must of necessity meet the Rushmores everywhere. Do you even know what the reason is for the hostility?'

She was asking because Rupert had regretfully to decline an invitation, having already been promised to their common neighbour.

'Lost in the mists of time,' Edward said. 'I believe it was something to do with the Civil War. We Marchams remained loyal to the Crown. The Rushmores went with the Roundheads.

145

I believe it was all very bitter at the time.'

'But that was nearly two centuries ago! What can have been so bad as to continue through the ages?'

Edward looked at his daughter. 'In truth I don't know, but I believe it was more to do with Simon Marcham and the Rushmores' daughter than who favoured which side.'

'You don't know and yet you continue to cut them?'

'It has become a habit,' he said with an edge to his voice.

Phoebe could hardly believe she had all her life accepted the feud without question. But with the round of visits since her aunt and her cousin had come to stay, it had been forcibly borne upon her that there were things to which the Marchams had not been invited. She had herself of habit excluded the Rushmores from her own invitations.

What interested her more, though, was this new information regarding Simon. Could this be the true love spoken of in his poem? She felt both excitement and frustration. Snippets of information kept coming to light, but it was even more of a puzzle than the maze which stood in the grounds. A puzzle she was more determined than ever to solve.

★　★　★

'You are well-acquainted with Hugh Rushmore, are you not?' Phoebe asked Rupert when they were attending yet another picnic.

'Hugh? Yes, he is a particular friend of mine.'

Rupert looked uncomfortable, aware of the antipathy between the two families. It was inevitable that the Marchams and Rushmores meet occasionally. They were always meticulously polite, but that was as far as it went. Phoebe and Hugh had observed the feud simply because it was the way it had always been. She could see now how absurd it was.

'I should like you to arrange for us to meet.'

'Dash it, Phoebe, why can't you write him a note yourself?'

'I cannot ask him to Glendale. My father would not like it. Nor can I invite myself to his home. I would like to meet him on neutral ground.'

'If you ask me, the whole thing is very silly.'

'I can only agree, and cannot believe I have gone through my whole life without questioning. Dearest Rupert, do me this favour if you will. I promise I will not cross swords with Hugh.' She smiled appealingly, her dark eyes glowing.

Rupert, never able to resist his friend when she was in teasing mood, agreed to arrange such a meeting if Hugh was willing, 'though for all I know he feels as strongly as both your parents and may not even consider it.'

'We can but try. I must try.'

11

On the third day after Duncan had arrived at Kirkleas, his sister-in-law returned home with her son. Malcolm had only recently attained his second birthday, along with the ability to walk; an attribute of which he was immensely proud. Unca Dunca was adjured to watch his progress across the room from his mother's knee to his father's. The effect was a little spoiled when, having triumphantly reached his destination, he turned to see if his uncle was still watching and promptly fell to a sitting position. His little face began to crumple, whereupon Duncan jumped from his seat, swept his nephew high in the air and praised him for being a very clever boy. The threatened tears abated and Malcolm giggled instead.

'You have a way with children, I see,' said Jane. 'Few men so large have that gentleness which both you and your brother display.'

Duncan had liked Jane on sight and had lost his heart entirely to Malcolm. There was a new softness too about Fergus. Duncan experienced a pang, if not of envy, then certainly something akin to it. He thought about Phoebe every waking hour. Though he didn't know it, he had had the same argument with himself as Phoebe had undergone. He reasoned that with her open and friendly manner, there was nothing to indicate whether or not she had a preference for him above any other. That she enjoyed his company was undeniable, but she enjoyed the company of others also. Having at first resolved to put her out of his mind, he decided instead to write to her.

My Dearest Miss Marcham,
Forgive my presumption in writing to you, but as I had to take my leave in such haste I would like to explain the situation more fully now. My

mother is gravely ill. She grows weaker every day. You are aware that our relationship is not what I would have wished. I cannot, however, leave her now, and must in any case be bound here for some time, as there is much to do after so prolonged an absence.

He paused for a moment to glance out of the window where his brother was balancing Malcolm on the back of a tiny pony, Jane standing to one side and smiling. Duncan sighed and continued.

While I do not leave my mother's side for long, I have had an opportunity to inspect my overseas purchases. Some pieces are very beautiful (I would love you to see them) but none is more moving than that of Simon and his love. I am sure you are continuing your search and I wish you every success. I would, if permitted, like to join you at some future time to aid you if I am able.

With affection, Duncan Armstrong.

Duncan had chosen his father's library in which to write his letter. How well he remembered his father placing him on top of the steps. The little boy he was then had clung in fear to the pole. In flashback he could feel his own face crumple and how his father had swung him in much the same way as he had recently swung Malcolm. A rumble of thunder disturbed his reverie and told him the impending storm was moving closer. He sealed his letter and went to sit with his mother.

⋆ ⋆ ⋆

Phoebe, receiving Duncan's letter in due course, was frustrated to say the very least. What did *bound here for some time* mean? A week? A month? A year? And then . . . *like to join you at some future time to aid you.* Time again, but how long? Just as Phoebe had begun to get used to his absence, Duncan had crept in again beneath her defences. *Well I won't have it! I shall get on with my search and I shall get on with my life!* And she swept out to meet Hugh Rushmore.

Rupert had been as good as his word, and the two were to meet at Cranford. Looking somewhat forbidding, he was standing by the fireplace as she entered the room with her friend, who then excused himself. Undaunted, Phoebe approached Hugh without constraint, offering her hand in greeting.

'It was good of you to agree to see me. I can well imagine my father's sentiments if he knew of this meeting; yours also. And perhaps you, too, feel the same,' she said, her voice raised in question.

He took the proffered hand, and though he didn't quite smile, his features softened. 'It would have been rude of me to refuse your request. In truth, I was curious to know how I could be of service to you. I admit to being more than a little surprised.'

'And who can blame you? The situation between our families is not a happy one. I would choose to change it if I can.'

'To what purpose?'

'If for no other reason than it must be uncomfortable for our hosts when we meet in their homes. There is, is there not, always an undercurrent, polite as we are to each other.'

'I have to admit it had never occurred to me. You are right, of course.' He paused to offer her a chair. 'Is there anything else behind your desire for a reconciliation?'

She smiled broadly, surprising him into responding, for there were few who would not react to Phoebe's open and friendly countenance.

'Am I so transparent? I meant what I said about our neighbours, truly I did. But yes, there is more. I have of late taken a greater interest in my own family's history, and find that the feud between the Rushmores and the Marchams dates back some two hundred years. My father is quite hazy about its origin, and I was hoping you or your father might be able to shed some light on the matter.'

Hugh doubted there was any chance of gleaning information from his parent, for if he spoke of the Marchams at all it was always with loathing. He decided honesty was the best policy.

'The likelihood of my father cooperating in such a venture is small, I fear.'

'Mine too, I think.'

'I am happy to search our archives at home to see what I can uncover. It would be good to lay this ghost to rest.'

Phoebe looked up, startled until she realised the reference was allegorical. They agreed to meet again in a week to see if either had made any progress. Hugh rose, and it was he this time who offered his hand.

'I am grateful to have this opportunity of expanding upon our relationship. I look forward to our next meeting.'

Phoebe was satisfied. Upon Rushmore's departure, she thanked her friend profusely for his help and returned home to continue her search.

'I cannot express sufficiently what a treat it is to be once more out of doors. Wiggins has been doing her very best to entertain; but much as I admire Lord Byron, I can listen no longer to her reading of *Childe Harold*, as it makes me restless.'

'Well I am delighted you are able to venture out, Aunt, and cannot comprehend why we didn't think before to obtain a wheelchair for you.'

'And the doctor has told Mama that she might soon attempt a few steps with the aid of crutches,' Lydia added.

All three ladies were seated on an area of lawn where a table and chairs had been placed in anticipation of a visit from Rupert and Max. Upon their arrival Sir Edward joined them and tea was served. They had an unobstructed view across the parkland.

'I hardly know which way to look, I have been confined within the house for so long,' Sophia said without complaint but merely to express her delight. 'Your gardeners are very talented, Edward. I particularly admire the way they have shaped those two bushes in the form of a peacock, and feel I could pluck one of the feathers to adorn my bonnet, so real do they appear.'

Sophia Talbot, it seemed, was a changed woman. It might have had something to do with her release from enforced confinement, but it was becoming increasingly evident that there was a growing intimacy between herself and Max Brendon. If anything were needed to soften her mama towards Rupert, Lydia conjectured, it was her own attachment to his father. Not that Rupert had declared himself, but Miss Talbot was beginning to hope. Yes, definitely she was beginning to hope.

Dear Mr Armstrong, Phoebe wrote, for the circumstances of his mother's illness made it only polite that she respond to Duncan's letter. *It was* kind of you to write and apprise me of your circumstances. May I express my deep regret at your mother's illness, and hope she is not greatly suffering. Regardless of your previous sentiments, it is to be wished there is yet some affection that can bring comfort to you both.

I suspect, having observed you at Glendale, that you experienced a good deal of excitement when reviewing your own collection. My search here continues. But of course, you do not know! I have found the goblet! You may well imagine my feelings when I discovered it hidden in a secret compartment in my mother's desk. Sadly I have made no further progress. You will remember Simon's poem, I am sure. However, that which is engraved inside the goblet is none other than the family coat of arms! You may imagine how many times it appears, both within and outside the house. I am in despair of even finding the right

location, but shall continue as before. Should you ever have the opportunity to return to Glendale, no doubt I shall still be at my quest.
Phoebe Marcham

There, she thought, I have left things quite open, though I no longer anticipate his return. That was what she told herself, at least; but it did not preclude hope.

★   ★   ★

Duncan's mother passed away the day before he received Phoebe's letter. It had been a quiet passing, her sons both with her and each holding her hand. Duncan had very mixed feelings. Though he could never forgive, he had, over these two weeks, become accepting. His instinct upon receipt of the letter had been to head straight for Somerset. This giant of a man had lost his mother — twice, in his opinion; and his twin, always so close, had found happiness in another quarter. Duncan, ever before in control of his destiny, craved the comfort of the woman he loved. Vulnerable as he was, however, he resisted the temptation to pack his things and leave. What if she rejected him? A fine fool he would appear. What chance was there that she might have developed those deepest feelings on such short acquaintance, never mind that he had?

He stayed in Scotland, but only with the express purpose of settling his affairs. He and Fergus held the property and land jointly, but his brother had his own family now. The estate was large and wealthy enough for them to sell, albeit reluctantly, some of the farms and associated assets. He hoped Fergus would be happy to dispose of them to purchase his brother's share. Kirkleas was no longer large enough to hold him.

'You cannot mean that,' Fergus had expostulated. 'This is your home!'

'Be honest if you would, Fergus. This

hasn't been my home for many years, not since I went to university. And even before then, since our father's death, it has never meant as much to me as to you. Why then would I have travelled all these years? No, it is time. Nothing will ever sever the bond between us; but if you think I'm going to live under the same roof as you, you may think again. You would forever be playing off your tricks on me, just as you used to,' he said with a broad grin.

Fergus smiled back at him. He knew his brother well enough to know there would be no turning him once his mind was made up. 'Very well. We must get our man of business to sort out what we should sell and what is best retained. It will take some considerable time though, I think. Will you remain here meanwhile?'

'I said I would no longer live with you. I did not say I wouldn't visit. Yes, of course. In any case, I need some time to develop my relationship with my nephew. I would not want him to have forgotten me when I return to see you all again.'

Both men felt lighter once the decision was taken. Harder would be the arranging of their mother's interment.

12

'I thought I might approach my father first as we were looking at family portraits,' Hugh said when he and Phoebe next met to discuss their ancestors. 'It seems the antipathy between our families stems from the time of the Civil War. Mine were staunch supporters of Cromwell while yours remained loyal to the king. Though there was much bitterness between the warring factions, it turns out ours was more personal than that.'

'You know it to be so?'

'Yes, for my father led me to a likeness of a young girl. Agnes Rushmore was only fifteen when it was painted, and she died the following year. Her death was, and still is, blamed on her association with Simon Marcham.'

'So we know the origin but not the reason.'

Hugh smiled, evidently pleased with himself. 'Ah, but my conversation with my father was not my only attempt at getting deeper into the background. As promised, I began a search of our family archives — and look what I found!' he said triumphantly, bring forth a volume he had previously held hidden away.

'What is it?' Phoebe asked excitedly.

'It is Agnes's journal!'

'And it contains information about her and Simon?'

'Assuredly it does.' Hugh opened it at a page he had previously marked. 'See here. These are the first references I found.'

'My family have forbidden me to meet my true love. I shall not heed them. I shall not!'

'This wretched war is driving people apart. They shall not come between Simon and me.'

'Mama has told me I am too young to understand what love is, but she

was married to my father when she was but sixteen, as I am now.'

'I don't know how I shall sleep tonight. Simon has asked me to meet him tomorrow in Glendale's home wood. Dare I go?'

'Our love is true. We carved our names upon a tree. It will forever be our special place.'

Phoebe judged it to be time to tell Hugh about Simon's poem, and now laid it before him. He read it, looked up at her questioningly then back at the paper.

'You have searched for this tree?'

'A few times, when on my morning ride. I think Jester must wonder at my odd behaviour, asking him to stop at the most unlikely places instead of allowing him a good run. The home wood is extensive. The tree may now be covered in ivy. I place little hope of finding it that way. Surely Simon must have left some other clue, or Agnes.'

'I will carry on searching at home.

You must let me tell you, Miss Marcham, that even if our search proves to be fruitless, I am glad that between you and I at least the feud is over.'

'And I, Mr Rushmore. It has continued far too long.'

*   *   *

Lydia was beginning to wonder if her heart had led her astray. Rupert was as attentive as ever, but no more so it seemed than with the other girls. Could she have been mistaken? Was what she had seen as becoming particular in his attentions merely an extension of their friendship as they became better acquainted? There were times when he looked at her warmly, but she feared now she was reading more into it than she ought.

She would have been more than reassured had she known Rupert's feelings. Aware that she was for the time being a captive at Glendale, what might happen, she wondered, if he declared himself and she rejected his offer? How uncomfortable it would be for Lydia if she didn't return his sentiments and was obliged to see him almost every day? So Mr Brendon was biding his time, not the pain he was causing the one he loved.

Lydia resolved to take the problem to her mother. 'You will have noticed, Mama, that I am less than indifferent to Mr Rupert Brendon,' she said, blushing slightly. 'I have no way of knowing, however, if my sentiments are returned. Do you think I should distance myself a little?'

Sophia laughed, a trill girlish sound that had been rarely heard in recent years. 'By no means, my dear. I am as certain as I can be that Mr Brendon has every intention of making you an offer — if you would but give him a little encouragement.'

'Encouragement! But I have given him little else!'

'In your eyes, perhaps. But you are a

modest girl and unused to putting yourself forward.'

'I hope I have behaved only as you have always taught me,' her daughter replied, a little shocked. 'And in any case, Mr Brendon seems to show me no particular preference above the other young ladies of his acquaintance.'

'And indeed how could he? He has been raised as a gentleman. It would be ill-mannered of him if he treated them differently. But I have noticed a warmth in his eyes when his gaze falls upon you.'

'Do you think so, Mama?' Lydia was a little breathless.

'I have always been truthful with you, Lydia, and it would be unkind of me now to raise your hopes if I believed them to be unfounded.' She paused before continuing. She did not wish to distress her daughter, but the time had come for her to unburden herself. 'There is only one thing in all your life that I haven't been entirely honest about. I must tell you father and I were never really suited. I was not fortunate enough to have the same understanding with my own mama as I believe you have with me.' She squeezed her daughter's hand. 'When Talbot was presented to me as a suitor, I felt it my duty to marry to oblige my family. I had formed an attachment to another, but it was not to be. My parents told me in no uncertain terms that the man of my choice did not match their expectations for me. Talbot knew my heart was given elsewhere, but he was ambitious. In society's eyes, ours was a good match. You have yourself received two altogether eligible offers, but I knew your feelings were not engaged. If I seemed at first to be a little distant towards Mr Brendon, it was because I needed to be sure of your sentiments. You must follow your heart, Lydia, for to enter into a loveless marriage is not what I would choose for you.'

Lydia was stunned. Her father had always been a distant figure, but she had had no conception that her parents' marriage had not been a happy one.

'I see you understand,' Sophia continued as Lydia pressed the hand that was holding hers. 'It may be that Mr Brendon has never lost his heart before. It is my belief the depth of his affection for you has taken him by surprise and he is uncertain whether or not to proceed.'

'Do you think so, Mama?' Lydia said again.

'I am as certain as I can be. Therefore, while I would not wish you to behave in any way that offends your principles, I feel that a little less caution on your part might be beneficial.'

Sophia waited some moments for her words to take hold. She had done all she could. It was up to her daughter now.

'Be a good girl, will you. Find your cousin and ask her if she has a sketchpad or watercolours I might make use of. Now that I am able to venture into the grounds, there are many things I would like to capture if I might.'

Lydia, her head in a whirl, went off to find Phoebe.

*   *   *

Duncan was captivated by his nephew, and if anything could have held him in Scotland it would have been Malcolm. But his thoughts of Phoebe were paramount. The task involved in cataloguing his collection would be time-consuming; but one night, lying sleepless on his back and thinking of Simon Marcham, it occurred to Duncan there was nothing to stop him interrupting the work and going to Glendale for a week or two. The prospective journey was not daunting to one who had spent years travelling in Europe; and Rupert, he knew, would accommodate him, for his friend had thrust an open invitation upon him.

'Any time, old man. You know you're always welcome here.' For the first time in weeks, Duncan slept through the night.

* * *

'I will return soon. I promise.'

Fergus chuckled. 'It would serve you right if I had the whole lot broken to rubble and used to pave the garden paths.'

'You are barbaric! These are works of art, not lumps of old stone.'

'Don't worry. I shall keep them safe for you.'

Duncan chose to travel by coach, having decided to take a small statue with him as a gift for Phoebe. It was of a horse, and the sculptor had captured the flaring mane and tail of a stallion at full speed. Other than professing a desire to see Rupert again, it was his feeble excuse for the journey.

Taking leave of his family with some regret, he whiled away the time thinking about his future. He realised he would shortly be homeless and would have to purchase a new property. His reasons were threefold. He had no desire to hire someone else's house. His collection needed a permanent home, a large home! The overriding factor, though, was that he hoped to make Phoebe his wife. Should she accept him, they would need somewhere to live, and he knew she would not wish to move any great distance from her father. And what of Simon? Their search might continue for many years. No, it would be necessary to remain close to Glendale.

With these happy thoughts running through his mind, the journey passed otherwise uneventfully. The letter he had sent ahead to Cranford would warn Rupert of his impending arrival. But how he would be received at Glendale exercised his mind considerably. The devil in him had asked his friend not mention his impending return. He planned, the morning after his arrival, bold as you please, to invite Phoebe to ride with him as they had done before.

Phoebe and Hugh had met once more at Cranford and, while nothing further came to light, each was gaining a better understanding of the protagonists. They met also at a soirée given by Mr and Mrs Fairweather, and Harriet was astonished to see them in close conversation.

'I have something to show you that I think might be of interest,' Hugh was saying. 'Are you able to meet me at Cranford on Wednesday? I have asked Rupert, and there can be no objection.'

'Then of course I shall come. Would the afternoon suit you?'

'Certainly. Say, at three o'clock?'

'I shall look forward to it.'

★ ★ ★

'So you see, we shall glean no more from Agnes's journal, but this last entry is telling indeed.'

Phoebe stared at the page in frustration.

'I am to be torn away. They are determined to separate us, and I am to go to my father's sister. My faithful Mildred takes a note to Simon, for I must see him one more time to explain ... and to say goodbye. I fear the storm, but I must go.'

'Oh poor child; and how brave!'

'I wonder what happened when they met. I cannot believe Simon would have accepted his fate so readily. Moreover, I would have thought their love so strong he would have run away with her,' Hugh said with a frown.

'But we know he did not, for it was he who found her body. Something must have happened in the storm. I shall have to search further among my mother's papers. I am inclined to go back to the beginning, now that I have some small idea of what I might be looking for.'

'Do let me know if you discover anything, and I shall do the same,' he said as he held the door open for her.

She pulled up short, a gasp escaping her lips, for who should be entering the hall from the front door but Duncan. Rupert had received his friend's letter too late to cancel Hugh and Phoebe's meeting without seeming to be rude. He couldn't believe that fortune would arrange for all to be there at the same time.

Duncan was as taken aback as Phoebe. However, there was nothing for it but to press on.

'Miss Marcham, it is a delight to see you again. I am, as you will observe, just this moment arrived. With your permission, I shall call on you tomorrow to see how your aunt does,' he said, one eyebrow raised.

Phoebe bit her lip. He had not lost the ability to make her smile instantly, and she well knew that the niceties of enquiring of her after her aunt's health were entirely out of character.

'I am sure she will be only too happy to give you a detailed account of her progress,' she replied, the bubble of laughter rising up into her throat. 'You know Mr Rushmore, I believe.'

'Of course. We have met many times,' he said, shaking the other's hand. 'How are you, Hugh? And your father?'

'Both well, thank you. I have it from Rupert that your mother passed away. Please accept my condolences.'

'As to that, she would only have suffered had she lingered. She is at peace now,' he said, remembering her demons and hoping they had been laid to rest with her, and thinking of Simon and knowing his hadn't. 'Please excuse me. My man has taken my things upstairs and I must see all is to rights. The same room as last time, Rupert?' he asked, turning to their host.

'Yes. Come, I will take you up. Phoebe, I will arrange for someone to escort you home. I know Rushmore would not be welcome.'

This time she did laugh, a delightful chuckle that Duncan remembered so well. 'You may be sure of that. I expect my father would turn me off if I brought the enemy to the door.'

★ ★ ★

Rupert and Duncan climbed the stairs together, Rupert apologising and explaining his predicament. Duncan made little of it. He was more concerned about the extremely cordial relations between Phoebe and Hugh. Were they not sworn enemies? What had happened to bring about such a closeness between them? When he had seen them together, his heart had sunk, and it was still lying somewhere in the pit of his stomach.

The following day, wishing to bestow his gift upon Phoebe, Duncan chose not to have Beau saddled up but instead borrowed Rupert's gig. He could not know she had waited expectantly for him and had kept Jester delayed far longer than she liked before riding out on her own. Duncan didn't put in an appearance until the afternoon, when he was shown on to the terrace, where her aunt gave him just such a comprehensive account of her progress as Phoebe had foreseen. Sophia was not complaining, but instead was full of praise for everyone's aid in her recovery.

'I use the crutches still, for I am not steady on my feet yet; but as you can see, I am in fine frame.'

'My aunt has certainly healed since you last saw her, Mr Armstrong.'

'Indeed; I am hoping she will honour me with a dance at Brendon's reception in a couple of days.'

Sophia laughed delightedly and rapped his knuckles with her fan. 'Foolish boy. I do not dance, but it is kind of you to flatter an old lady.'

'There was no flattery intended. I am certain you would not be susceptible to such treatment.'

'But which you would no doubt engage in if you thought she would,' Phoebe said with what could only be described as a grin.

'Naturally. I may be many things, but not, I hope, a fool. I wonder, would you mind joining me for a moment in the yard? I have brought something with me about which I would value your opinion.'

'Of course,' she said, rising and leading the way. 'I had no expectation of seeing you again in Somerset.' She paused, allowing him time to draw level with her. 'I am glad you were able to reach your mother in time,' she said warmly. 'No matter the differences between you, I am convinced it will have been a comfort to you both.'

'You are right, as ever. I must return to Kirkleas before long, for my circumstances have changed . . . ' He paused, unsure how to continue. The perceived closeness between Phoebe and Hugh had altered everything in his mind. Overnight he'd had time to consider what he had seen and had ascribed it with far greater significance than was there. Forgetting that Phoebe's manner with all was open and friendly, he had attributed her ease with the other man to an intimacy he had hoped was exclusive to him. He had been about to tell her that one of his reasons for coming south was a wish to see her again. Now somehow it seemed inappropriate. ' . . . but I have some business here that I first need to attend to.'

She was too polite to ask what.

'Ah, here we are,' he said, lifting the statue from the gig. He placed it on a small table he had asked Will to bring into the stable yard. 'There! What do you think?'

'He is beautiful,' she said, enraptured. 'May I touch him?'

'Of course.'

She ran her hands over the shoulders and the back. 'Look how the sculptor has captured every muscle and sinew. And the mane! The tail! He is exquisite.'

'I am glad you like him. He is for you.'

'What? No, I couldn't possibly accept.'

'Well now, I'm in a quandary. What is left for me to do then but to carry him all the way back to Scotland?' he said, eyes once more alight with laughter.

'But I couldn't,' she said, more hesitantly now. 'Could I?'

'I can think of no reason why not. In fact, in my mind's eye I have already allocated what I believe will be the perfect place in the Long Gallery.'

'Oh no, I would have him in my dressing room,' she said, blushing even as she spoke. 'Then I shall see him every day, for I do not go to the gallery every day.'

'Then you accept. I am delighted.'

'I shouldn't, I know. But yes; and thank you.'

13

'What a slow top you are, old boy. I felt sure you would have fixed your interest with Miss Talbot by now. What are you waiting for?'

Sitting on the terrace at Cranford in the fading light, Rupert blew a cloud into the air and watched it dissolve into the shadows. 'I feared to put my luck to the test in case she might refuse me.'

'Well you won't know unless you try.'

'No — don't you see? While she is confined in Somerset, just think how uncomfortable should she not return my affections, when we are obliged to meet nearly every day.'

'Whereas you will wait until she leaves and the opportunity will be gone. And from what I saw of Baroness Talbot today, that time will not be long in coming.'

'I don't know. Sometimes I think she

will look kindly upon my suit. At others I see her with the likes of young Wainwright and believe she treats me no differently from him.'

'What, that sapling! Lydia will always be kind and polite, whether her affections are engaged or not. Go to it before she leaves the district.'

'You are right. I shall declare myself immediately.'

'I doubt you will be welcome at this time of night,' Duncan said, for it seemed Rupert was indeed ready to call for his horse at that moment.

Both laughed and went later to bed, the one in the hope his offer would be accepted, the other despairing that he was regarded only as a friend by the woman he loved.

*   *   *

Phoebe was nervous the next morning, not sure if Duncan would ride over as before. She needn't have worried. He arrived in good time, and they trotted towards the wood before Phoebe called to him and reined in, a question on her face.

'I was wondering, now the weather is kinder, if you would choose to ride about the estate.'

Duncan was in two minds. Was she trying to avoid the easy conversation they were used to having in the clearing? He could not know, but was certainly interested in seeing more than just the land that immediately surrounded the house and said so. They set off at a walk, Phoebe telling him they would soon have the opportunity for a good gallop. The vista presented to him was of rolling hills, the scenery quite breath-taking.

'You are lucky indeed to live in such a place. Where I come from, the terrain is more rugged. It's beautiful in its own way, but very different from Somerset.'

'I should love to see it. I have never been to Scotland.'

'I will take you one day,' he said in his straightforward manner, but she laughed and told him he was being foolish in the extreme. Duncan felt rejected. Phoebe pointed and said the land in that direction belonged to the Rushmores.

'One can see how close is this part of our neighbours' domain to our own home wood. I have been discussing Simon and Agnes's story with Hugh Rushmore. It's what we were doing when you arrived this time at Cranford.'

'Agnes?'

'Simon's sweetheart. We have discovered much in your absence.'

Duncan, while delighted at the outcome, was not best pleased at the way it had come about.

'But of course! We have not talked about the mystery since your return. I have so much to tell you. Would you care to remain for a while after our ride, and I will show you all?'

This was sounding better. Duncan gave himself over to the enjoyment of the ride and the anticipation of what was to come.

* * *

Paying his final visit to make sure all was now healed, the doctor arrived at Glendale to see Baroness Talbot at exactly the time Rupert rode over from Cranford. By sheer good fortune, Rupert found himself alone with Lydia on the terrace. He wasted no time in declaring himself.

'Lydia, my darling. Your mother is now well, and I fear you are about to be taken back to London.' He threw himself onto one knee and grasped her hand. 'You must know of my sentiments. I would make you my wife. Please, Lydia, say you will marry me.'

This rather dramatic proposal did nothing to diminish Rupert in Lydia's opinion. He was her knight in shining armour. She drew him to his feet and looked up into eyes that were filled with hope.

'It is my dearest wish to be your wife, Rupert. Of course I will marry you.'

He clasped her in his arms, she

covered in confusion but oh so willing, before they strolled about the terrace, both in a state of heightened tension. Wanting badly to share their joy, they had to wait for the doctor to leave. Fortunately they did not have to wait long. Sophia joined them outside, exclaiming that the doctor had declared all was well and she might now resume life as before.

'But what is this?' she exclaimed, observing Lydia's hand clasped tightly in Rupert's. They sprung apart immediately, but only so that Rupert could address the older woman.

'Your daughter has done me the honour of accepting my offer, Baroness Talbot. We are hopeful you will give us your blessing.' Rupert was a little nervous but dogged nonetheless.

'Give you my blessing! Of course you have it, dear boy. And you, Lydia — I could not be happier for you. Come now, give me a hug.'

This startled Rupert, for it was addressed to him. Then into this happy scene walked Phoebe and Duncan, who had just returned from their ride. Phoebe was delighted for her cousin, and the immediate celebrations overtook their intended pursuit. Agnes and Simon would have to wait for another day.

*　*　*

The family dined alone at Glendale that evening. Lydia was at first uncomfortable at finding herself to be the centre of attention. Discussion of her forthcoming marriage soon led her to relax, however; and even Sir Edward, who usually did not take a deal of note about these things, was delighted.

'I have become very fond of you, my dear; and it will be a comfort to Phoebe, I know, to have you living so close.'

His words were meant well, but there was a slight pause after he spoke. With her daughters married in close succession, it might be anticipated that Sophia would be lonely in London without the two of them. Talk fell quite naturally into plans for the future, and Sophia expressed a need to return home, 'for there is much to do. Well, I daresay I shall be as exhausted as I was by your sister's wedding, Lydia. Do you not recall how many visits we paid to this shop and that; the purchase of silks and muslins? And then the fittings necessary to make all perfect.'

'How could I not, Mama,' Lydia said with a smile. 'And the milliners. Such delightful confections. The bonnet I had from Miss Starke in Conduit Street is still my favourite.'

It was at this point that Sir Edward lost interest, so the ladies left him to his port and continued the discussion in the drawing room.

'I envy you. I had little opportunity for shopping when I came to visit before, though I must say I am delighted with my riding habit.'

'Come with us! Oh do come, Phoebe, if Mama should not object,' she said, looking at her parent in case she had been presumptuous.

'Mama most definitely does not object.' She smiled serenely upon them.

'So, Phoebe, will you come?'

Phoebe looked from daughter to mother and back again. It would be fun, wouldn't it? It would do her no harm, either, to buy some shoes and a reticule or two for herself. She made up her mind.

'I shall be delighted. When do you plan to go?'

*   *   *

'So although Mr Rushmore retains the journal, I have copied out the entries I consider to be relevant. Here they are,' Phoebe said, laying the paper on her mother's desk for Duncan to see. Both were still in their riding clothes, Phoebe having invited him into the house the next day following their morning ride, which they seemed to have resumed as a matter of course.

'My family have forbidden me to meet my true love. I shall not heed them. I shall not!'

'This wretched war is driving people apart. They shall not come between Simon and me.'

'Mama has told me I am too young to understand what love is, but she was married to my father when she was but sixteen, as I am now.'

'I don't know how I shall sleep tonight. Simon has asked me to meet him tomorrow in Glendale's home wood. Dare I go?'

'Our love is true. We carved our names upon a tree. It will forever be our special place.'

'And this last one is the final entry.'

'I am to be torn away. They are determined to separate us, and I am to go to my father's sister. My faithful Mildred takes a note to Simon, for I must see him one more time to explain ... and to say *goodbye. I fear the storm but I must go.'*

'And no-one saw her again alive?'

'No. It is understood that Simon found her body. But why was he not there to meet her, Mr Armstrong? Tell me that if you can.'

He couldn't, of course.

'It is my intention to search my mother's box more keenly now that I have more idea what I'm looking for. I said as much to Mr Rushmore.'

Rushmore again. Duncan, who had liked the chap before, was beginning to hate the sound of his name. He berated himself for being a fool and again offered to help Phoebe with her search, 'for two heads are better than one.'

'Well I should appreciate your assistance; there is much to go through. I will have little time as well in the foreseeable future, as I am to go to London with my aunt and cousin.'

This came as a shock to Duncan. Had he come all the way from Scotland only for Phoebe to remove herself from the area?

'I had observed, of course, that your relationship with your aunt has improved beyond recognition. Do you plan to make a long stay?'

'As to that, I cannot tell you. Lydia asks me to go with them to aid in the purchase of her trousseau. I am hoping also to enjoy a trip to the theatre and one or two other things I was unable to do on my last visit.'

Duncan asked when they would be going.

'Within two or three days, I believe. Lydia and Rupert are anxious to wed as soon as possible. I know not whether he will join her in town or if they are to be married at Cranford.'

Conversation ceased as they set aside Phoebe's notes and concentrated on their search. They began with the lowermost document in the box, laying it face down and examining the next, and so on. Duncan found it hard to focus with his mind on other things.

14

'Things will seem a little flat without the Glendale party, don't you think, Rupert?' Duncan asked his friend at breakfast the next morning.

'No such thing, for I plan to go to London myself. I have been meaning to go for a while, and this will be as good a time as any.'

'Nothing to do with the fact that you cannot bear to be parted from the fair Miss Talbot?' Duncan teased.

'And so what if it is? You could do worse than to find yourself a nice girl to settle down with. It would do you no harm to put down some roots.'

That there was nothing he desired more, Duncan did not confide in his friend. With Phoebe going to town, his dream seemed further away than ever. 'Stay as long as you like. Max will be glad of the company, but I know you'll understand why I wish to go.'

'I remember the last time I was there. Do you recall? It was near the end of term and we were sent down for some childish misdemeanour, both of us. You were terrified that Max would be displeased and withdraw your allowance, so we bolted to the city instead. Lord, what a time we had. I have a fancy to see how it has changed.'

'Well of course! Why ever didn't I think of that? You shall come with me!'

'Just what I was thinking myself. I shall write to Fergus that I am further delayed.'

'Yes, do that. I must write also; send an announcement of the betrothal to the *Morning Post*. Lord, doesn't that sound grown up!'

'Well it's time you did.'

'Yes, old man.' Both laughed out loud and went about their various tasks.

* * *

Duncan was surprised to receive a note from Phoebe at around midday. They had ridden that morning as usual, and he'd had no expectation of seeing her until the following day; so when he read *Please come this afternoon if you are able, I have something I would show you*, his curiosity was considerably aroused. He went straight away to tell Rupert where he was going. His host, anxious to see Lydia, kept him company, 'for they leave in two days and we cannot follow immediately, as I have one or two commitments here.'

They joined the ladies in the drawing room at Glendale. Phoebe asked to be excused, and withdrew with Duncan to her mother's sanctum.

'So after I returned from our ride this morning, I changed quickly into my day dress. I was anxious to look once more at the papers while I still have the opportunity.'

Duncan made no mention of the fact that he too would be going to town, as it was obvious she had something of great importance to tell him. His news could wait.

'Tell me, what have you found?'

'It's in Simon's hand,' she said, passing a sheet of paper to him. 'We missed it before because it was stuck to the back of another document. I think age and damp must have welded them together. Only as I turned it over to lay it face down could I see what appeared to be a wrinkle at the edge, but which turned out to be this,' Phoebe said, pointing dramatically to the document in Duncan's hand.

I know not how I shall survive this day. I had been away from home and returned to find Agnes's maid waiting for me. She was extremely anxious and had been here above two hours. 'My mistress bade me give this into your hand, sir,' she said, and left. Agnes asked that I meet her in our usual place. A storm had blown up and I raced from the house, fearful that she had been for so long at its mercy. My fears were only too well founded. My beloved is dead,

*taken by our very own tree, which
had been struck by lightning and cut
her down. I blame myself: had I not
been from home, I might have
received her note in time to prevent
such a tragedy. I carried her broken
body back to Glendale, and she is
with me now. I write this as I wait for
her family; I have sent them a
message and expect them at any
moment. Oh Agnes, my dearest girl,
how shall I live without you?*

Duncan raised his eyes to see
Phoebe's own filled with tears.

'It is no wonder he cannot rest,' she
said. 'He feels responsible for her death.
It is probably just what he told her
parents. In their grief, I can imagine
how they censured him. It would have
been enough to confirm his guilt in his
own mind. We cannot know for sure, of
course, and I doubt Simon will have
written of this again except for his
poem, which he has left as a clue. I shall
continue searching, but I fear we will

find nothing more.'

'I think you are right. Will anything be gained, do you think, from noting all the places your family coat of arms appears?'

'A hopeless task! It is everywhere. No wonder the secret has never been disclosed,' Phoebe said.

'You will not give up?'

'Never. I promised him, you see.'

It was obviously still not the time to tell Phoebe that he too was to go to London.

★　★　★

'Rupert has just shown us a copy of the notice he has today sent to the *Morning Post*,' Lydia said when Phoebe and Duncan returned to the drawing room. 'I cannot believe that I will be Mrs Brendon in just a few weeks,' she added, her cheeks becomingly flushed. 'We are to be married in London, for Clarissa and her husband reside there and Max has expressed a willingness to undertake the journey. If you are not called back to Scotland, Duncan, perhaps you will be able to remain until the wedding. I would have you play the role of best man.'

'I should be honoured to do so. I have already advised Fergus that I do not know when I shall return.'

'Then it is settled.'

Phoebe looked from one to the other. There was a realisation that Armstrong's presence would greatly increase the enjoyment of her own visit, for it could not be imagined that she would not see a great deal of him.

'Are either of you familiar with the capital?' Sophia enquired. 'My son-in-law is a member of White's and visits many other gentlemanly establishments unknown to us. I am sure he will be more than happy to show you the way.'

'We would be grateful indeed, Baroness Talbot. I was saying to Mr Brendon only this morning that I haven't been to London since my university days, and I daresay much will have changed.'

'Where do you plan to stay? I take it you do not have a house in London.'

'No indeed. Mr Armstrong and I shall engage rooms at Fenton's Hotel or perhaps Grenier's, but we would certainly be grateful for any assistance from Mr . . . erm?'

'Sir George. Sir George Denby,' Sophia said, preening a little.

'We would be grateful for any assistance Sir George might be able to render us,' Rupert said. There was no need to inform his future mama-in-law or indeed his bride that they were hoping to visit Jackson's Saloon for a little sparring or indulge in some fencing if the opportunity was to be had. Women were strange about these things, and he thought it best not to mention them.

Duncan smiled at Phoebe as they left. 'And you will meet me tomorrow as usual? It will be our last opportunity for some time.'

'Of course. I shall look forward to it.'

*   *   *

The ladies had departed for London a few days earlier, and Duncan and Rupert were having a quiet game of cards at Cranford with Max and Edward. The convivial atmosphere altered somewhat when Hugh Rushmore was announced, and Sir Edward rose without exchanging greetings, and with apologies to his host said it was time for him to leave.

'I am so sorry, Rupert. Had I known Marcham was here, I would never have come. It is the same with my father. I just pray that ultimately Miss Marcham will be able to bring about a reconciliation.'

'What's that? Reconciliation? You must be all about in your head if you think that will ever happen,' Max snorted.

'No such thing, Father. Phoebe is doing her utmost to discover the reason for the rift and hopes to bring to an end this two-hundred-year-old feud. Isn't that right, Duncan?'

'Yes; she has discovered some clues amongst her mother's papers and is closer to a solution, I think.'

'I hope I have been of some assistance; I was able to furnish her with some of our own documents. Not that I mentioned it to my father.'

'I believe Miss Marcham hasn't informed Sir Edward of your meetings either. Well, Hugh, now that you are here, would you like to take his place at the card table?'

'Don't mind if I do.'

Duncan and Rupert were for a while able to put their respective ladies out of their minds; and when Max retired to bed, the three younger men abandoned the cards to enjoy some whisky Duncan had brought with him from Scotland. With Phoebe so many miles away and Duncan not for the present seeing Hugh in the role of rival, they spent the time in good humour until the early hours.

The next morning Rupert awoke

with a severe headache, much as he had on his friend's previous visit.

'But I do not complain. The whisky was excellent!'

★ ★ ★

The ladies, meanwhile, were settling into the house in Chesterfield Street. The journey had been tedious, and poor Lydia had taken to her bed and was still to be found there with the shutters drawn. All changed the following day when Clarissa paid them a visit. She was not accompanied by her husband; and Lydia, though still pale, sent her maid to the morning room with a message begging her sister to remain, for she would get dressed and be with them in no time. She was as good as her word; and after the two girls embraced, was adjured to lay on the couch with her feet up. Clarissa, it seemed, had news.

'I waited until you were home. I wanted to tell you in person.' She turned, wide-eyed, to Sophia. 'Mama, Lydia, Phoebe . . . I am with child.'

She laughed as Lydia attempted to exchange places with her.

'I am not ill, dearest. In fact, I have never felt so well, and seem to have acquired a new level of energy.'

'Well if you do not do as your sister says, you will obey your mama at least, and I am telling you to sit down,' Sophia said sternly to cover her emotion, though nobody was fooled for one moment.

'Here, Mama, take this,' Clarissa said, removing a handkerchief from her reticule and passing it to her parent, who took it gratefully, laughing and sniffing at the same time.

'Well I never. One daughter in the family way, another soon to be married. What a year this is turning out to be.'

'I think, dearest aunt, that it is perhaps you who should be reclining, for you are clearly overcome,' Phoebe said with a laugh. They sat, all four, and

Sophia was heard to remark several times, 'Well I never, well I never.'

★ ★ ★

During the coming days, the carriage was called for several times to take the ladies shopping. The proprietors of the several establishments that enjoyed their custom remembered Baroness Talbot well; she had spared no expense in purchasing the best for her elder daughter some few months previously. They were assiduous in their attention and knew well how to assess their clientele. While she demanded assistance, Baroness Talbot was not one who liked to be fawned upon. One lady, overly anxious to please, made the mistake of commending her taste in a way that Sophia found unctuous in the extreme.

'I shall not be shopping there again, you may be sure,' she told Lydia. It was with no little regret that the crepe was left behind, together with that young lady's vision of how it might look when made up.

'Do not distress yourself, my dear. We shall find something you admire just as much, I am sure.'

'Yes, Mama.'

Phoebe was also able to indulge herself, and commissioned several gowns and hats to be made. Towards the end of their first week in London, the ladies received a visit from Mr Brendon and Mr Armstrong. Both thought what a lovely picture Phoebe and Lydia presented, the dark curls of one mingling with the blond ringlets of the other as they pored over a book of dress designs.

Sophia was absent from the room, so Rupert wasted no time in clasping his betrothed's hands in his own and declaring, 'Lydia, my days have been empty without you.' He was rewarded as the pressure on his own increased and she gazed lovingly into his eyes. Duncan wished he might similarly have been able to greet Phoebe, but instead was confined to exchanging the usual pleasantries.

'I trust you are enjoying your visit,' he enquired, looking at her in that warm way that had drawn her to him from the very first moment they had met.

'Immensely, and I fear I shall have to hire an extra carriage to take my purchases when I return home. Do you look to replenish your own wardrobe while you are here?'

'And how am I to take that? Do you consider me so badly turned out that I must at once do something about it?'

She chuckled back at him and gave him his own. 'Do you then consider that I have been so badly turned out?'

'Touché. Yes, I am hoping to add a few items while I am in town. Certainly I need some new boots.'

'Will you stay for tea? I shall ring for a tray.'

'Thank you. You are very kind.'

The bubble of laughter that seemed always so near to the surface when she was in the company of this man rose again. 'I try when in the presence of others to remember my manners.'

'You do it very well. And when you are not in the presence of others?'

'Ah, then I may be as hoydenish as I please and none to care.'

'Good afternoon, gentlemen,' Sophia said, entering the room. 'It is a pleasure to see you. We have been looking for you these two or three days now. You will stay for tea? Phoebe, do please ring for a tray.'

Phoebe and Duncan exploded into laughter, and it was some time before they were able to apprise the rest of the reason for their merriment.

15

'For such a large man, you are light on your feet, sir,' John Jackson said to Duncan. Not everyone who visited the boxing salon at 13 Bond Street had the privilege of going a round or two with the great man himself, and Duncan was well aware of the honour conferred on him.

'I haven't been to London since I was a cub at university, Mr Jackson, and I wouldn't then have had the temerity to ask you to stand up with me. I am happy to say you have today helped me to fulfil a long-held ambition.'

'You could do better with regular practice, but I could see as soon as I set eyes on you that you'd strip well, else I would've passed you on to another.'

'I am well aware of the concession and can only offer my gratitude.'

'No need. You're welcome to come

and see me again while you're in town.'

Had Duncan been a smaller man, he might have been knocked off his feet by the gentleman who rushed passed him in the doorway as he left. As it was, he just looked a little surprised and raised one eyebrow at the retreating back of his assailant. Duncan strolled the short distance to Fenton's Hotel, where he was to meet Rupert.

'You'll never guess who I just bumped into. Or rather who bumped into me, on the steps of Jackson's salon. Fingers Fawley, would you believe!'

'Well I never! What did old Fingers have to say for himself?'

'Nothing. He was in far too much of a hurry to pass the time of day. I'm not even sure he recognised me.'

'Now you're gammoning me. There ain't many men of your size walking the planet.'

'Well he chose not to anyway. I can't say I'm sorry. I still regret the loss of that fob, and unless it fell down an unseen crack there's no-one else who could have taken it.'

'If you'd been the only one, I'd have said you'd imagined wearing it that night. Besides, had that been the case, it would have still been in your room. He didn't acquire his nickname by accident, did he?'

'No; but it's so many years ago now that perhaps he's changed his ways. Anyway, tell me how you got on with the ladies,' he said, happy to turn the subject.

Duncan was fond enough of Rupert to listen to his raptures without complaint.

'We are to be married in three weeks. If it weren't for those wretched banns, I would have it sooner, I can tell you.'

'When does Max arrive?'

'Oh, my father won't be here until a day or so before the wedding. Town life don't suit him, and I have no doubt he will return to Cranford as soon as he can.'

'And what are your plans? Will you be taking your bride to visit all your friends, or to the continent now that it is safe to travel there?'

Rupert smiled. 'Since when did you think I had a notion to go gadding about, in this country or any other? You're the one who likes to be on the move. To tell you the truth, Lydia doesn't travel well and would prefer we go home as soon as may be. But the thought of leaving her mama is troubling her, I think. I was wondering whether I should offer to house the baroness as well!'

'Are you insane, man? Do that and you will never be rid of her.'

'Well I can't say the idea appeals to me, and Lydia hasn't herself suggested it; but it seems cruel to leave her in that big house on her own.'

'I think you will find she has enough to occupy her with her other daughter who lives close by. You would do well to propose that she comes to you for an extended visit next summer, since there's no doubt she was pleased to be out of town these last couple of months. And in any case, how do you think such a suggestion would go down with Max?'

Rupert grinned. 'I don't think he'd object too much. Quite taken with her, he is, ever since the time they played piquet together at Glendale. Wouldn't surprise me if he made such a suggestion himself.'

'Don't do it, Rupert.'

'Perhaps I won't. It don't stop me feeling guilty, though.'

The two friends parted company for long enough to change their clothes. They were to join the ladies for a light supper prior to visiting the theatre.

* * *

The Denbys welcomed their guests to Covent Garden, where Sir George hired a box for the Season. Lydia was joined at the back of the box by her sister, who declared that Shakespeare's tragedies made her feel morbid and she couldn't wait for the farce to begin later in the evening. Phoebe had little opportunity as a rule to partake of a pastime she greatly enjoyed and sat staring at the stage, watching the drama unfold before her. Duncan's attention was focused as much on her as on the play.

'I have to say I am exhausted merely watching them,' she declared during the interval. 'And even though I know the ending, I cannot wait to see the rest. How the actors keep it up for so long I don't know. It was kind of you to invite me, Sir George.'

'I am delighted at your pleasure, Miss Marcham. Clarissa is not much addicted to the play and enjoys much more the social aspect of attending the theatre.'

'It is of all things the one I most miss on account of living in the country, though I have several times visited the Theatre Royal in Bath.'

'I was privileged to see Rossini's *La Cambiale di Matrimonio* while in Venice a few years ago,' Duncan said. 'Are you a devotee of the opera as well as the play, Miss Marcham?'

'Assuredly. You must know, Sir George, that Mr Armstrong has journeyed widely abroad and has entertained us on several occasions with his descriptions of things he has seen.'

'You must consider me a coxcomb. Am I so full of my own conceit that I bore you with my experiences?' he asked, but his eyes were smiling.

'Not at all. You must have noticed surely how I hang on your every word,' she said, reflecting his humour. 'Come; we must be seated again. I believe the next act is about to begin.'

'Then I trust you will enjoy it as much as the first and will join us again when we make up another party.'

'Thank you, Sir George. I should be delighted.'

* * *

Things were a fair way to being in place for Lydia and Rupert's wedding, so the ladies were free to entertain themselves during the days approaching the nuptials. These were to take place in St George's Church in Hanover Square. One day in early October, it being cool but pleasant, Phoebe and Lydia took the carriage to Green Park. They were strolling in the afternoon sunshine when they were approached by a well-dressed gentleman who claimed Miss Marcham's acquaintance.

'I doubt you will remember me. But I had the pleasure of meeting you some months ago. You were in town for your cousin's wedding, I believe.'

'I was, sir, though you will have to excuse me. Your name for the moment escapes me,' she said, straightforward as ever.

He laughed in appreciation. 'I had the pleasure of standing up with you at Almack's. Frederick Fawley at your service.'

Phoebe did not find the man encroaching. His manners were as plain as his dress, neat to a pin but with no ostentation. Had he pressed her, she would have withdrawn; but it seemed he was ready to move away when he said, 'I see you are still at a loss, so I shall trouble you no further.'

Perversely, Phoebe chose to extend the encounter. 'No, I am pleased to have the opportunity of renewing our brief acquaintance. Allow me to make known to you my cousin, Miss Talbot, with whom I am staying at present.'

'Good day, Miss Talbot,' he said, bowing over her hand. 'But forgive me, were you not staying with Miss Talbot when last we met?' he asked, turning to Phoebe.

'I was indeed, Mr Fawley, but it was my cousin's sister who was then to be married and is now Lady Denby. I am in London now because Miss Talbot's own wedding is approaching and I am to attend her in church.'

The gentleman turned once more to Lydia. 'My felicitations. Is your wedding to take place soon?'

'In less than two weeks. Mr Brendon sent a notice to the *Morning Post*, but perhaps you overlooked it.'

'Mr Rupert Brendon!' Fawley exclaimed.

'You are acquainted with him?'

'Yes, though I haven't seen him for years,' he said in a quieter tone. 'We were at university together. Well, I wish you every happiness, Miss Talbot. I hope, Miss Marcham, to have the honour of standing up with you again soon. Good day.' And he was gone as quickly as he had appeared.

'Was that a bit strange, do you think? His manner changed completely when you mentioned Rupert's name. I wonder what it was all about.'

'He did seem to take his leave rather abruptly. And I think we too must take ours, or Mama will be wondering what has become of us.'

* * *

Frederick Fawley was indeed distracted as he walked away. He had been delighted to see Phoebe, recognising her at once as the heiress he had met earlier in the year. Things were not going well for Mr Fawley, and he had a while ago concluded his only salvation lay in taking a wealthy bride. He would, however, have liked also to be able to admire his chosen wife, and that had not proved to be so easy. Desperate as he was, he had not been able to bring himself to offer for a single one of them.

But he remembered Phoebe from their previous encounter. As well as being very beautiful, she was also quick-witted and able to hold an intelligent conversation. That she knew Brendon was not helpful. The two men had not been friends, and Fawley felt Rupert held him in contempt. Perhaps there would be a way of separating Miss Marcham from the happy couple. He resolved to further his acquaintance with her.

★ ★ ★

Phoebe was sitting in the morning room with her cousin when Frederick

Fawley was announced. She looked up, surprised.

'Good day, Miss Marcham. Miss Talbot. I trust I do not come at an inconvenient time.'

'Not at all. We are alone for the time being and glad of company, both my mother and my fiancé having deserted us,' Lydia said with her ready smile. 'Would you like some refreshment?'

Fawley accepted the offer and began to ask the bride about her forthcoming nuptials. There was no doubt he had a certain address, but Phoebe could not like him. Too practised. That was the conclusion she came to; and in the following days she found nothing to change her mind. He visited often; and following his first call, he made Phoebe the object of his attention. On two occasions he found Rupert and Duncan before him and didn't linger.

'I see you do not admire my new suitor,' Phoebe said in an undertone when Rupert was engaged in conversation with Lydia and Sophia. Her eyes were laughing, but it seemed Duncan did not appreciate the humour as she did.

'Is he annoying you? Give me the word and I will see he doesn't call again.'

'No, how could you? This is not my home, and it is not for you or me to dictate who calls.'

'Tell me truly, does he make a nuisance of himself?'

'As to that, no; but he is a little more forward than I would have him be on such short acquaintance.'

Duncan forbore to remind her he had himself been excessively forward from their first meeting onwards and she seemed not to have had any objection there. The reflection gave him hope. He had a pressing problem. The wedding was to take place three days hence. If Brendon was to carry his bride directly to Cranford, Duncan would need to find other accommodation. Still, he feared to put his luck to the test. That Phoebe liked and trusted him, he knew; her confidences about Fawley proved that. But he couldn't get out of his mind her easy exchanges with Hugh. Did she not appear to treat them the same?

He was still procrastinating when he walked into the Talbots' morning room to find Phoebe alone with Fawley and struggling in his arms. All consideration of keeping his own counsel fled as rage overcame him. With no thought but to relieve her of this imposition, he pulled the offender away and planted a right hook of which Jackson himself would have been proud.

'I'm sorry. I didn't mean ... my feelings overcame me,' Fawley said, scrambling to his feet. 'I will take my leave of you,' with which statement he glared venomously at Duncan and withdrew. Neither Phoebe nor Duncan noticed; she was overcome by fury, and he, mistaking her tears for fear, enveloped her in his arms and murmured in her ear.

'There, there, my darling. Don't cry.

I shall never allow that blackguard near you again.'

She looked up into his face. What could he do but kiss those trembling lips?

'I thought you were my friend,' she said, the first to recover.

'I am your friend, but I desire to be so much more. Miss Marcham, will you do me the honour of marrying me?'

'Only so that you will remain at Glendale to help me solve Simon's riddle,' she said, smiling. 'We will stay at Glendale, won't we? My father . . . '

'I haven't told you, I think, that I have sold my share of Kirkleas to my brother. You find me homeless with no roof to call my own.'

'Why, then, can I see a smile in your eyes?'

Duncan explained with all due modesty that he was in fact a very wealthy man. He would not remain at Glendale as her pensioner; some arrangement must be made. But neither would he tear her away from her home and her father. Where, in any case, could he take her?

They were discussing the possibilities when Lydia and Rupert came into the room. One glance was enough for them to sum up the situation, and a toast was drunk to the happy couple. Sophia, when she joined them, was delighted, going so far as to joke that she could now be happy to see them ride out alone together.

'You will stay with me for a short time after Lydia and Rupert return to Cranford, for you will need to buy your own bride clothes, and I would be happy to assist you.'

It was a command rather than a request; but Phoebe, her relationship with her aunt now being far more amicable, was more than willing to acquiesce.

'Had you not offered, dear aunt, I would have asked. Thank you,' she said, taking Sophia's hands into her own and clasping them warmly. 'Your taste is impeccable. I have seen as much when shopping for my cousin.'

Baroness Talbot was affected in no small way, happy to have at last reached an understanding with her niece. She hid her feelings in bluster, remarking that she must bustle about; for Mr Brendon, the elder Mr Brendon, was due to arrive later in the day in time for the forthcoming nuptials, and she had much to do. No-one was fooled, however. Sophia had softened beyond recognition.

16

'Aunt Sophia, have you seen my locket? I seem to have mislaid it, though I cannot understand how as it is forever clasped about my neck except when I am asleep.'

'Your mother's locket?'

'Yes, and the most precious thing I own. I can only assume it must have dropped off somewhere in the house, as I haven't been outside since I put it on this morning.'

'How distressing for you. I remember Emily's joy when our own mother gave it to her on the occasion of her wedding. I have one very similar.' She paused, obviously listening. 'Is that a carriage? It would seem Mr Brendon has arrived. I shall ask the housekeeper to instigate a search before I go to greet him.'

Phoebe was more upset than she

cared to show. Her father had given her the keepsake after Emily's funeral. 'Look after it well, my child; and remember, while you wear her locket your mother will always be with you.' She had searched the morning room and her own bedchamber. Could it have come off when Duncan had embraced her?

She sent a message to Fenton's Hotel, where he had said he was going upon leaving her, and he returned immediately, but without the news she'd been hoping for. He exchanged greetings with Max, recovering from his journey by taking refreshment in the morning room with his hostess. A comprehensive search of that room was conducted, but to no avail. The response from the servants too had been negative. It seemed Phoebe's treasured possession was lost, perhaps forever.

★ ★ ★

Frederick Fawley arrived back at his rooms in deep despair. While Phoebe had given him no particular encouragement, her manner had led him to believe he might have a chance with her. She was not, after all, in her first or even her second Season, and must surely be wanting to establish herself. Foolishly, he'd concluded that Miss Marcham was to be his salvation.

He raked his hand through his hair and was surprised to see something dangling from his cuff. Close inspection revealed it to be Phoebe's locket. It must have torn off when he was struggling with her. He took it between finger and thumb, and he could see this was no trinket but rather a valuable piece of jewellery. He considered his options carefully. Should he return it to her? No, he decided. All he would gain was her gratitude.

He turned his mind to how he could best profit from the situation. He could sell the locket, of course, but he wouldn't receive anything like its true value. Another far more loathsome solution occurred to him. He availed himself of paper and pen and began to write. He decided to allow Phoebe time to realise and rue her loss. She would be frantic to know its whereabouts and would pay handsomely to retrieve it. The locket was engraved not with her name, but he was familiar enough with her circumstances to know who Emily was. With a sneer that distorted his features, he folded the note, placed it on the table ready for later, and went out with more of a spring in his step than had been apparent for some long time.

★ ★ ★

On the eve of the wedding, Max and Duncan bore Rupert off, and Phoebe was grateful to enter with Sophia and Lydia into those last minute arrangements, as they helped take her mind off her loss. They were disturbed early in the afternoon when a footman knocked discreetly on the door.

'A note for Miss Marcham. Said it was urgent, so I brought it straight up.'

'Thank you, Simpkins.'

The words were scrawled — Fawley had made some effort to disguise his hand — and appeared to be from someone with little education. She sat down, pale at first, and then with heightened colour as her anger rose.

'What is it, my dear? Have you received bad news?'

'No, Aunt. It seems my locket has been found, and that cannot be bad news. This person,' she said, waving the note in the air in disgust, 'demands a ransom for its return. You will not believe the price he asks! I shall not pay. How dare he!'

Sophia pointed out that if she did not pay, she was unlikely to retrieve her property.

'It is repulsive. Excuse me, but I must leave the room; I can see I am distressing you. Do not worry. I shall think of something.'

Alone in her bedchamber, she read again. She was to come unaccompanied to a designated place at five o'clock that afternoon. If anyone was seen to be with her, the deal was off. If she followed instructions, her locket would be restored. There was some suggestion that she might arrive in a hackney, which could wait for her at the end of the alley.

Phoebe, far from being afraid, was determined the villain should not be allowed to get away with it, but she was at a loss to think of a solution. Yes, she was a tall woman, but she didn't feel confident about tackling a grown man on her own. In the end she decided she must enlist Duncan's help. She had no hesitation asking him. Her worry, as she hastily wrote a message, was that it might be difficult to find him in time. She had no idea where three high-spirited men out for some fun might go to find suitable entertainment. Her mind was quick, though, and she remembered that Max had brought his valet with him from Somerset. She sought him out and he undertook to carry her note to Duncan without delay.

Phoebe returned to the morning room.

'Are you all right? What have you decided?'

'Do not worry, Lydia. All is in hand. Now tell me, what is it to be? The ivory ribbons or the pink?'

*   *   *

Phoebe made no attempt to see her bank manager. There was no way she would succumb to blackmail. As she waited, it seemed the time dragged interminably as she prayed Duncan would receive her message and come to her aid. Just as she'd decided she must call a hackney and go alone, he rushed into the house.

'What is it?' he asked, all concern, for there had been little in her note other than a call for help. 'What has happened?'

'You'd best come with me into the library and I'll explain.'

She had never seen Duncan angry before. It showed him in a new and, under the circumstances, not unwelcome light.

'You are dressed for the street! You were about to go alone? I cannot believe you would be so foolhardy.'

Naturally this did not go down well, and her own temper flared. 'Would you have me then ignore the summons entirely? I have no address; just an alley. If I do not go, my mother's locket will be lost to me forever. How could I know you would be here in time?'

'I am here now. Go back to your aunt. I will deal with this.'

'You cannot have thought. One look at you and the villain will run away. I have to get near enough that he doesn't suspect. If you would but remain hidden until I have made contact, I am sure you will be able to overtake him.'

Duncan could find no fault with Phoebe's plan, and a hackney was summoned. They spoke little during the journey, but Duncan held fast to her hand. He felt uncomfortable hiding himself as Phoebe stepped from the carriage, but he had no choice.

As she entered the alley, a figure appeared at the far end. She moved slowly, hoping her adversary would walk towards her and thus be closer when Duncan made his move. He came a short way and stopped. In an obviously disguised voice, he called for her to come to him.

'You will understand, I am sure, that I do not wish to venture far from my cab. I will come no further. Here — I have what you asked for,' Phoebe said, holding out a bag stuffed with paper. 'Let us get this over with quickly so I may never see you again.'

Greed made Fawley over-eager. He moved forward. Duncan leaped from the carriage and was upon him before he realised. Kneeling on his stomach, Armstrong tore off the kerchief that had been hiding Fawley's face.

'You! I knew you capable of villainy, but never suspected you would stoop so low.' So saying, he hauled him to his feet and tied his hands behind his back, using the very same kerchief he had whipped from his face.

'My locket, Duncan. Does he have my locket?'

He'd almost forgotten Phoebe, so great was his disgust. He put his hand into Fawley's breast pocket and retrieved the jewel. At least Fawley had intended to fulfil that part of the bargain.

'I have it, Phoebe, and I apologise, but I must request that you sit in the cab with this filth until I have handed him over to the law.'

Fawley, still dazed from the blow, went meekly enough, knowing that he would never again be accepted in society; that a prison sentence awaited him; that his life was ruined. As he cowered in the corner, Duncan turned to Phoebe and tenderly clasped the locket around her neck, back where it belonged.

Lydia's wedding day dawned bright and sunny. Baroness Talbot sat in the front pew, Clarissa on the one hand and Phoebe on the other. If the older lady shed a few tears, it was not to be commented upon. A small number of guests marked the occasion, joining the family for a wedding breakfast before Rupert and his bride set out for Cranford. Max was to remain in London for a few days, and removed to Fenton's Hotel, but both he and Duncan spent much time visiting the ladies.

It was during one such visit that Max asked to see the sketches and watercolours Sophia had executed when staying at Glendale. Duncan took each in turn and held up the work for all to see. As he displayed one of the sketches, Phoebe gasped and clutched her hand to her locket, a sure sign of her agitation.

'What is it, my dearest?' he asked and

she pointed to the drawing. 'What? What have you seen?'

The image Sophia had chosen to depict was of the old ice house, unused for decades. But in spite of foliage having grown about its entrance, the Glendale coat of arms was clearly visible through a gap in the ivy.

'What do you think? Is it possible?' Phoebe asked, wide-eyed.

Duncan's eyes were as alight with excitement as her own. 'You're thinking . . . '

'Yes, a secret passageway.'

'Whatever are you two talking about?'

It was time to fill them in a little on the details.

'So you're saying that Simon's clue leads you to the ice house.'

'It's a possibility, don't you think, Max? A way he could come and go unnoticed. And if there is a passage, what better way for the lovers to meet in secret?'

'When can we go, Duncan? I'm sorry, Aunt, but I cannot delay if there is a possibility we might solve the mystery.'

'I perfectly understand. Indeed, I am myself excited, and hope that my meagre artistic efforts may be significant.'

'I cannot stay at Glendale. It wouldn't be appropriate. Not until we are married.'

'You will come to Cranford with me. The place is huge. We need not inflict ourselves on the young couple,' Max said, coming to the rescue.

Sophia was looking dejected.

'And you shall come with me to Glendale, Aunt Sophia. Clarissa's confinement is not for some time. It would be a shame if you were not able to join in the adventure, since you have had such a significant part in it now.'

'I would like that very much.'

And so it was decided.

17

The party broke their journey overnight and stopped the next day for an early luncheon before arriving at Glendale in the middle of the afternoon. The gentlemen, pausing only to exchange greetings with Edward, continued on to Cranford, with Duncan promising to return early next day to continue their search. The baroness allowed herself to be fussed over by her old nurse; and Phoebe, restless and not the least bit tired, could hold herself no longer.

'It serves no purpose for me to wait. I shall see you later,' she said to her aunt, who was so engrossed in conversation that she barely looked up to acknowledge the comment.

Armed with a torch, Phoebe pushed at the door of the old ice house. It resisted but gave way under pressure. Phoebe, finding herself in a large chamber, was convinced it had been used centuries earlier as a place to hide from the Roundheads, well before the custom of storing ice in this way had come into use. But if she was right, why would the Glendale coat of arms have been flaunted at its entrance? Perhaps it had been constructed for some entirely different purpose, or the embellishment added later. Had her ancestors taken refuge here in harder times? She felt a sudden rush of cold air, though the flame on her torch remained steady.

'Simon?'

Any doubts she may have had at once disappeared. Simon seemed to lead her to the side of the chamber. She held the torch close but could see nothing significant. Then, as she ran her hand over the wall, there was a perceptible change in texture and temperature. She found a hidden opening, partially obstructed, that reached just above waist height. Shielding her torch, she pushed hard against the blockage. It was as well she did, for it gave way against her weight and a rush of air nearly extinguished the flame.

She could feel the cold that was Simon move ahead of her into the tunnel, and without hesitation she stooped and followed, heedless of the centuries of dust and dirt that dirtied the hem of her gown. The floor sloped gently downwards, and Phoebe moved as quickly as she could; for her great great great — however many greats — grandfather was obviously after all this time in something of a hurry.

She ran on for what seemed like an age until suddenly she tripped over a protruding root and tumbled headlong, banging her head as she fell. The last thing she did before losing consciousness was to whisper, 'It wasn't your fault, Simon.'

★ ★ ★

Sophia didn't think much about Phoebe's absence for some while. However, the days were drawing in now, and as dusk settled she stirred herself and went in search of her niece. She was nowhere to be found. Edward had seen her only briefly upon their arrival and the servants not at all. Worried now, Sophia suddenly remembered Phoebe's parting words. Something about not waiting. She'd spent enough time with her niece over the past few months to hazard a fair guess as to what that might mean. With increasing concern, she sent a hastily scrawled note to Duncan. He came immediately to find the baroness pacing up and down.

'What did she say? Do you remember?'

'That it would serve no purpose for her to wait. That she would see me later. I didn't give it a thought, Mr Armstrong. I was talking to Mrs Wiggins and not really paying any attention. Do you really think she's gone to the ice house?'

'I would lay money upon it. But why has she not returned? You did right to send for me. Please excuse me; I must see if I can find her.'

'I pray she is all right.'

'As do I.'

Duncan raced to the ice house, and it was evident immediately that Phoebe had been before him. The entrance to the secret passageway was lit by his torch. He was grateful to find the tunnel quite roomy and hurried onwards, blood pounding in his ears for fear of what he would find. Eventually he came upon Phoebe, sitting up now and rubbing her head. Relief at finding her unharmed caused him to vent his anger.

'You could not wait! Were we not to look tomorrow? What would you have done if the ceiling had collapsed upon you?'

She looked up at him, tears glistening on the ends of her lashes, and he realised she had been severely shocked by her experience. Even by the light of the torch, he could see her face was ashen. He gathered her in his arms, soothing, apologising, and infuriated with himself that he might have added to her distress. After a while he felt her body relax.

'Can you tell me what happened?'

'He was here. Simon was here. He led the way. I tried to tell him that we'd found his letter. That we knew he didn't get her note in time. That he couldn't have saved her. Oh, Duncan, the torment he has suffered all these years.' Silent tears coursed down her cheeks. 'We have to go on. This will lead us to the answer.'

'We must get you home first. You need time to recover. We will come again tomorrow.'

'No, I am fine; and now that you are here, we shall do well. See, the ground begins to slope upwards again, which is the reason I think why I tripped on this root. We must be nearly there.'

He was about to protest when he felt — no, he saw — that Simon was with them. It was impossible to distinguish his features, but form and shape were definitely evident, and it seemed the apparition was leading them forward.

'Are you able to stand, Phoebe?'

'Of course I am. Come. We must go on.'

Duncan could see that some colour had returned to her cheeks, and so they followed where they were led. A few steps more took them to where the passage ended. Pushing brambles out of their way, they emerged into a clearing in the home wood. *Their* clearing in the home wood. *Their* tree.

'Oh Duncan, we were here all the time. This tree on which we have sat so many times is Agnes and Simon's tree. This is where they used to meet. But what of Simon's poem? Where are their names carved?'

'They must be on the underside or we would have seen them. Look, there is a gap underneath, here where the ground dips. If I could just crawl . . . ' he said. 'No, dammit, I cannot . . . ' But the apparition that was Simon could, swooping into the space beneath the trunk. They waited for some moments but he didn't reappear.

'I shall bring you back in daylight. We cannot scramble now on hands and knees to see. Come, let me take you home.'

* ★ *

Edward and Sophia were waiting anxiously when they returned to the house. The story was told, and Phoebe went to bed with some hot chocolate to calm her. She awoke the next morning as fresh as could be apart from a bruise where she had banged her head. Duncan was already waiting for her when she went downstairs, and Beau and Jester were saddled up and ready to go.

They didn't hurry. Keen as they were to confirm their conclusions, neither was in any doubt as to what they would find.

'How do you think the tunnel came to be there, and how did Simon find it, do you think?' Phoebe asked. 'Was it the war?'

'I imagine it must have been. An escape route for anyone wishing to flee the Roundheads. You remember how much hatred there was between your family and the Rushmores. The Loyalists were hounded to death. Many homes had hidey holes or tunnels at that time. Simon would have been well aware of it; would possibly even have ordered its excavation, though it must have been done in secret. I understand there were spies everywhere.'

'I'm proud of him, you know. What an ingenious way to meet his love undetected.'

'I can see I am marrying into a very resourceful family. What say you we give these two a chance to stretch their legs before we get there?'

They cantered along happily, side by side, until reining in where the trees were harder to negotiate, and finally arrived at the clearing.

'It looks the same as ever, Duncan. I

felt it might be different somehow.'

They began to move away some of the undergrowth that impeded their access, Duncan having had the forethought to have brought a knife. Finally they were able to clear a space large enough for his head, and laying on his back, he wriggled beneath the trunk. Phoebe was in a fever of anticipation, but he soon emerged with a smile as broad as any she had ever seen.

'It is there?' she asked breathlessly.

'Yes, and there is more. Newly carved beneath the rest are the words 'at peace'. It would seem he has taken our words to heart, and I believe he has left it as a message for us. I think we will not see Simon again. He is with Agnes now.'

*　*　*

By the time they returned to Glendale, the party from Cranford had arrived and were waiting eagerly for news.

'Aunt Sophia, I don't believe I have

shown you the statue of Agnes and Simon. It must have been carved sometime after her death, as Simon's father was still alive and would never have allowed it to be commissioned, let alone put on display.'

'Because of the feud?'

'Yes; a feud that continues to this day.'

She looked at her father from under her eyelashes, and it seemed that the barb might have hit home — particularly when the baroness exclaimed, 'But that is nonsense. Maybe not then, perhaps, for it was the way of things. But now? Surely long enough for any family hostility.'

'You are right,' Edward said. 'Do you think the Rushmores might be persuaded to visit so that we may discuss this sad tale and hopefully bring this ridiculous situation to an end?'

'The younger Mr Rushmore will come assuredly, for he has had no small part in helping to solve the riddle.'

'You have been in contact with him?'

Edward asked, incredulous.

'There was no way else we could proceed, and I had no argument with the family. Do you?' she asked roguishly.

'We have been foolish indeed. See then if you can convince the elder to join us with his son, and we will thrash this out once and for all.'

'And in the meantime, my dear, I should like to see the statue you spoke of, for I have heard so much about the young lovers I should dearly like to meet them, if only in stone.'

'Come then, Aunt, and I shall leave it to you and Rupert to engage with Hugh,' she said, taking Duncan's hand. 'Between the three of you, it shouldn't be impossible to pull it off.'

* * *

'I feel sorry for his poor wife, having to look at that every time she came in here. There's no denying the bond between the figures, is there?'

'It was a marriage of convenience I believe. Simon needed an heir and Lady Marcham was willing to comply.' Sophia winced. 'But I suspect my ancestor would have kept this statue hidden, because even down through the ages it is possible to see the family resemblance. There can have been no doubt who the subject was; but from all I can gather, Simon was a gentle man. I feel sure he wouldn't have flaunted his first love in the face of his wife.'

'A gentle soul indeed to have suffered so much for so many years.'

'You believe it then, this story of ghosts?' Lydia asked, astonished.

'What I cannot prove or disprove I can neither confirm nor deny. Your cousin's experiences and those of Mr Armstrong are too forceful to dismiss. And from what Phoebe tells us, my own sister had encounters with this spirit.'

'Indeed. Had it not been for my mother, we would never have solved the mystery. She would be glad I know to have been instrumental in all of this. As far as I can tell, she made it her life's work.'

'Well it is to be hoped the gentlemen are successful in convincing Mr Rushmore to bring discord to an end.'

And so it proved to be. Rupert returned to Glendale to collect his wife, and asked that the Marchams be expecting their neighbours the following afternoon.

Phoebe went immediately to tell her father. 'Harrumph!' was his only response; but it was obvious that he was at least ready to try and make peace.

18

Nine people assembled at Glendale the next day: Arthur and Hugh Rushmore and the party from Cranford. As for Edward and the elder Rushmore, there was goodwill and determination on both sides. Duncan was surprised when all were shown into Emily's private drawing room, for he knew it to be a sanctuary. But Phoebe and her father had discussed it earlier.

'This is as much your mother's concern as anyone's. She spent many hours there investigating, and it seems only right to me that the culmination of her endeavours should take place in this room.'

He nonetheless had to steel himself. As he moved forward, he ran his hand over Emily's desk; looked up at Simon's portrait on the far wall; turned to gaze at long-forgotten treasures, a trinket box he had given his wife on the birth of their daughter. All this time, Phoebe was settling their guests around the table. On it stood the chest with Emily's evidence, together with other items Hugh Rushmore had previously supplied.

'I think it best if Phoebe tells the story, as she has been the most involved,' Edward said.

'We all are aware that there has been a long-standing breach between our two families,' she began, addressing Arthur Rushmore. 'But in all my life it never occurred to me to question what it was until I discovered my mother's chest and found that its contents dated back some two hundred years. It is difficult, I know, for many to place credence in the reality of spirits, and I will not ask you all to accept what to me has been the unquestionable existence of Simon's ghost. However, there is written confirmation that it is impossible to deny.

'Agnes and Simon were young lovers. We learn from her journal that her family would not think about an alliance with its neighbours. An antipathy existed between the Protestants and the Loyalists at that time that could not be put aside for the sake of the deep affection between two people, she from one persuasion and he from the other. I once asked my father if he knew the reason for the enmity with Mr Rushmore, and he said it had been lost in the mists of time. Did you know this was the reason for the break?'

'No, I did not. Just that it had always been so and was insurmountable.'

'But is it insurmountable? Mr Armstrong and I have discovered that Simon believed himself to be responsible for Agnes's death, and doubtless transmitted his perceived guilt to her family. But Simon was not to blame. If blame can be attributed at all, should it not be to two stubborn families who strove to keep the lovers apart?'

Rushmore and Marcham looked guiltily at each other.

'It is evident my mother was not the

first to investigate what happened all those years ago. In the light of what she found, the clues that Simon left and extracts from Agnes's journal, I think we can say without fear of contradiction that the tragedy that occurred can be set solely at the feet of Mother Nature. Lightning struck the tree where Agnes was sheltering, and Simon could not have saved her because he did not know she was there. May we not now be grateful that the two are finally at peace?'

For a while there was silence in the room as Phoebe's tale was digested. Edward rang the bell, and a few minutes later a footman appeared with refreshments. It was Edward who filled the glasses and said, 'I think it is time we drank a toast to Agnes and Simon. I for one am proud of their devotion to each other.'

Arthur Rushmore reached for a glass. 'I too. I think today we have all learned a valuable lesson.'

The rest each took a goblet; and

Duncan, who had until now been uncharacteristically quiet, raised his and said, 'To Agnes and Simon. May they at long last rest in peace.'

'To Agnes and Simon!'

★ ★ ★

They all adjourned to the large drawing room.

'And I understand congratulations are also due to you, Miss Marcham, and to you, Duncan. I am delighted, for Rupert tells me you have deserted him to visit Glendale many times since coming to Somerset.'

'Ungrateful of you, Rupert, when all I was doing was exercising Beau for you.'

'Oh, was that it? And obviously, my own place not being extensive enough, you needed to ride over here to fulfil this favour.'

'Well, that and aiding Miss Marcham in her quest for a solution to the family mystery.'

'You are a complete hand, Duncan. Are you never without a ready answer?'

'Not if I can help it, Rupert,' he said with a laugh.

'Is your wedding to take place soon?' Hugh asked.

'As soon as it can be arranged. There is no reason to delay, and I daresay it won't be long before Rupert is wishing me elsewhere.'

'And while my aunt is here, she may remain until after the ceremony. It would be foolish for her to travel back to London, only to have to return in a few weeks.'

Their conversation was interrupted as Edward and Arthur rose to leave the room. Phoebe looked questioningly at her father.

'I am taking Rushmore to the Long Gallery so that he may see our statue of the young lovers. Naturally they have nothing like it at their place.' And off they went, leaving the rest to marvel at how quickly circumstances could change learned behaviour.

They returned some time later, and it seemed that Edward had tried to gift the statue to his neighbour, Arthur flatly refusing to accept. In the end they agreed that each establishment should house the piece for a year at a time, accepting that both had some claim to this part of their history. Another toast was drunk, and it seemed the two were well on the way to forging a firm friendship.

* * *

The next few weeks went by in a flurry of activity as arrangements were made for the wedding. Mrs Wiggins, delighted that her beloved charge was at last to be married, threw herself enthusiastically into organising the domestic side of things. Edward, enjoying the horse he had recently purchased from Max, drove himself over in the gig to visit the Rushmores. Both he and Arthur were doing their very best to make up for two hundred years of lost time, and so the only times Phoebe and Duncan could be alone were on their daily rides. They went still to the home wood, to the place that was ever likely to be a sanctuary for them.

'I cannot believe we have reached this time, Duncan. Tomorrow we shall be married.'

'And at last I shall be able to call you mine.'

'I have been yours, I think, since the day you unashamedly accosted me here. So large you were, and full of impudence. I did not know then that I would tumble headlong into love.'

'Whereas I knew immediately. I even told Beau of it as we returned to Cranford.'

She looked up at him, astonished. 'You did?'

'I have loved you from the moment we met. You make me laugh; you have never bored me, and only once or twice have you made me angry.'

'When? When did I make you angry?'

He looked down at her tenderly and

rubbed her cheek with his thumb. 'When you would face Fawley alone, and the day you entered the ice house without me. But my anger was born of fear. You are a courageous woman, Phoebe. It is one of the things I most admire about you. It shows itself even in the way you ride. And tomorrow we begin a great adventure.'

'Our marriage.'

'Yes, but that is only the start. I look forward to taking you to Kirkleas to meet Fergus and his family.'

'I am longing to see them, and to see where you were born and raised. If it is half as beautiful as you describe, it could not disappoint me.'

Duncan had spoken truly. It would indeed be a beginning, and for Phoebe the fulfilment of a lifelong dream. They were to travel from Scotland to France and onwards to Italy and Greece. The world she had always longed to see would be hers to explore. But for now, Duncan took her hand, kissed her fingertips, and helped her into the saddle. They rode side by side back to Glendale and forward into their future.

Other titles in the
Linford Romance Library:

HOLLY'S CHRISTMAS KISS

Alison May

Holly Michelle Jolly hates Christmas, and she has good reason to. Apart from her ridiculously festive name, tragic and unfortunate events have a habit of happening to her around the holiday season. And this year is no different. After the flight to her once-in-a-lifetime holiday destination is cancelled, she faces the prospect of a cold and lonely Christmas. That is, until she meets Sean Munro. With Sean's help, can she experience her first happy Christmas, or will their meeting just result in more memories she'd rather forget?